# Dear Billie

## Salvation in the Poconos

## Ben Miller

# Dear Billie
## Salvation in the Poconos

The events and conversations in this book have been set down to the best of the author's ability, although some names and details have been changed to protect the privacy of individuals.

First edition November 2018

*Edited by Andrea Miller*
*Cover Design by Ben Miller and inspired by God*

**ISBN 978-0-578-40143-0**

Published by Irving Spiff Publishing
Nazareth, Pennsylvania

# Dedication

This book is dedicated to my parents,
Alan and Sandra Miller. Your
unconditional love and support has
meant the world to me. I love you.

# Chapter 1

Dear Billie,

"Thank you" seems like the most appropriate way to begin this note, though it doesn't begin to convey the deep gratitude I'm feeling. I imagine that to you, my wife and I were just another couple, joining all the others who rented rooms at your inn this past weekend. The experience is a bit different on my end. You changed my life.

Our visit to Trakehner Inn began as a carefully crafted plan to surprise my wife with a birthday present she would not soon forget. I have been blessed by God in so many ways and Andrea is the proverbial gift that keeps on giving. I'm not entirely sure she isn't an angel in disguise, despite her prodigious talent for painting a verbal picture through profanity and clenched teeth. Five kids, two St. Bernards, and a husband like me will do that to anyone. The woman is a saint.

We met at one of the lowest points in my life, 12 years ago, when I had essentially given up hope for any sort of productive or fulfilling existence. I had consigned myself to the notion that I would never be truly happy again. I would go through the motions for as long as I was destined to trudge through the endless misery my life had become. Then, the release would come after I choked on my last breath and fell from this world into the next.

I cannot overstate how far down I had been pushed by life, or rather, by my own poor choices and the resulting consequences. When you think of people who hit rock bottom in a personal struggle or a particularly difficult time, they were standing on my shoulders, Billie. I had failed in every way imaginable, to the point that it became all I knew. I wrapped myself in a blanket of mortal obscurity and prayed for forgiveness from a God I felt had given up on me.

Hindsight lacks the myopia that comes in the moment and I can see now that I was the one who had given up on Him. I had been given chance after chance to change the course, despite my inability or unwillingness to embrace those opportunities. Then, I met Andrea, who was as stubborn as the day is long and had been beaten down by her own personal struggles.

We were working in a call center, her on the phones and me as a new hire, going through training. That job paid me a fraction of what I had made in previous positions and it was a giant step backwards in my career. Life had overcome me and accepting it was the ultimate sign that I had thrown in the towel. Yet, the seeds of my later success could only have been found there, buried deep within the heart of a golden-haired angel.

Andrea had no desire to meet anybody and wanted nothing more than to be left alone. I noticed her when my training class came out onto the call center floor because she had covered herself up under this little blanket and tried to blend in with the scenery. The more inconspicuous she tried to be, the more she stuck out from the others. When my instructor told me to sit with her, it went over about as well as loud flatulence at a funeral.

They called it a "ride along," new people sitting with seasoned representatives, listening to their interactions and learning from their experience. What I learned from my experience was that Andrea didn't like ride alongs and she especially didn't appreciate new people who insisted on trying to get to know her.

I should probably note that I hated the job, felt lousy about myself for taking it, and I wasn't the most professional fellow in the room. The more Andrea tried to shut me out, the harder I pushed back with personal questions and observations about the things around her desk. I had absolutely zero romantic ambitions, because the thought of someone like her with someone like me was absurd. Andrea was young and vibrant, with piercing blue eyes and a body that... well, she looked like a goddess. I, on the other hand, looked like a couple hundred pounds of a beaten old man, stuffed in some frumpy clothes and a pair of worn out sandals.

Oh yeah, the weight thing. You likely noticed that I've got a bit of a weight problem, by which I mean I weigh slightly less than your SUV. When I first met Andrea I wasn't as big as I am today, though I was still huge; My weight was closer to a compact car in those days. And before you think to yourself, "Aww, he's not that big," yes, I really am. I know thyself and thyself likes to eat.

There I was, sitting with Andrea, wearing a headset that allowed me to listen to her calls as she went about her job. At the same time, I was peppering her with questions like, "Why does this place always smell like cheese?" and "Do you have any tattoos?"

At one point, she tried to shut me up by letting me look through the items in her pocketbook. Didn't work. Finally, she relented and answered my tattoo question, telling me that no, she had none, but she found other people's tattoos interesting. That was the beginning of the end and it started a chain of events that turned an ordinary day into an unforgettable circus of absurdity.

What Andrea didn't yet know, was that I happen to have a tattoo of Sylvester the cat in a purple tuxedo, dancing on my left shoulder blade. So as not to leave you in suspense, yes, I was drunk when I got it. Judging by the looks of it, so was the tattoo artist.

When I told Andrea about my sly tattoo, she thought I was joking. That was my first glimpse at her smile, which was warm and inviting, and only encouraged me to go further. I insisted the tattoo was there and she shook her head, so I felt like there was only one thing for me to do. I began to take my shirt off, right there in the middle of the call center.

"What are you doing?!?" she gasped, as she grabbed my hands and tried to stop me. I told her I was going to show her the tattoo and feigned trying to pull off my shirt as she was pulling it back down me. That's when it happened. Andrea laughed.

I don't know if it was the thought of me actually having the tattoo or of me taking off my shirt in a crowded office, but she laughed and I could tell she wasn't prepared for that. Despite her best efforts to be annoyed and antisocial, she was having fun and the guy who had driven her crazy a few minutes earlier, was making her hold back an even heartier laugh.

In that moment, I felt something completely unexpected. Andrea had awoken feelings of joy that were long dormant and that laugh warmed me like a bowl of clam chowder on a cold winter's day. I was stunned and while I sat there contemplating the whole thing, wondering what to say or do next, a call came in on her phone line.

Andrea answered with the proper company greeting and was met with this question, "Hi. I'm a teacher at a school for students with special needs and I want to take my class on a whale watching boat ride. I wondered if it was ok to give them all sea sickness medicine before the trip?"

It was Andrea's turn to be stunned, considering those medications can have some pretty serious side effects and the teacher was thinking of dosing all the kids with no consideration for their medical history or parental consent. I slowly turned my head sideways towards Andrea, with a look of disbelief and my head cocked at an angle, the way a dog does when he hears a cat in the neighbor's yard. That's all it took for Andrea to lose it.

She fought like a champ to hold in her laughter to the point she was incapable of speaking, as tears streamed down her face. After what felt like a couple minutes, but was closer to 30 seconds, she hit the button to place the caller on hold, because she couldn't contain it anymore. I heard the phone line go silent and Andrea lose control, laughing hysterically, with the biggest and brightest smile I'd ever seen.

I laughed too, partially because of the madness in the caller's question, but more so because I had been swept up by Andrea's emotions. Her laughter triggered my own and as I sat there looking at her tears and that radiant smile, I felt happier than I had in years. It was as if I had been given a temporary release from all my own misery, to see what life could be like if I was willing to embrace it.

People around us were staring and one of the supervisors came over to make sure everything was ok. Andrea just shook her head as she continued to laugh. The supervisor then turned toward me and said, "You broke Andrea," before he walked away, shaking his own head, with a smile on his face.

Eventually, Andrea composed herself and went back to the teacher she had on the phone, apologizing for the abrupt hold. The caller was a good sport and laughed too, noting that she understood it probably sounded crazy. Andrea informed her that it was not a good idea to drug her students and then the call ended.

We laughed some more, joking about the call and the looks on the faces of the people around us. The grumpy, frustrated representative that I had been assigned to sit with had morphed in a stunning young woman, so happy and full of life. She seemed entirely unattainable, but at the same time, I was drawn to her and felt compelled to make her a part of my life.

A great friendship was born, and we gave each other our social media links and contact information for an online messaging program we both used. From that day forward, we talked whenever we saw each other at work and then later in the night, chatting for hours at a time through messaging.

Andrea is a great listener and I shared my story with her, both the good parts and the bad, because even after our strong connection, I never believed she would be interested in anything more than a friendship. Meanwhile, she was telling me her own story and flirting with me along the way, though I was entirely obtuse.

This went on for weeks until I realized that I had been wrong all those lonely years. I learned that somebody really could see beyond my faults and defects, that a woman as amazing as Andrea was not only able to look past my weight and medical problems, but was happy to accept me, no matter how damaged and flawed I felt I was.

We went on our first date to a local steakhouse and within months, we were making plans to get married the following year. Family and friends on both sides were surprised at how fast it had all gone and how well the two of us had meshed together. I genuinely believe that some things are preordained long before they happen and our relationship is most certainly one of them.

We were married in a pavilion on the beach in Cape May, with the Atlantic Ocean behind us and butterflies skirting through the dune grasses alongside the entrance. I'll never forget standing before our friends and family, fighting back tears as I waited for Andrea to arrive in her horse-drawn carriage. I was overcome by the moment and the sheer magnitude of our love, which was unlike anything I had ever known before.

Then, I realized I left my handwritten vows back at the hotel and I nearly cried for an entirely different reason. That was right about the time that the carriage arrived, the flautist played Pachelbel, and Andrea walked down the aisle. The minister quietly asked us if we had our vows, to which Andrea responded yes and I froze every muscle in my body, willing myself to become invisible.

"Tell me you're joking," she said.
"Uhhhh...," I responded.
"This isn't funny, Ben!" she sharply whispered.
"I left them on the table at the hotel. I'm so sorry."

It's been 12 and a half years of that, Billie, and she still keeps me around. Like I said, the woman is a saint. I really wanted to find some special way of showing her how much she means to me, which is why I booked our stay at Trakehner Inn on her birthday. I had high hope for this trip, though I never could have imagined the emotional journey that lay ahead.

## Chapter 2

Billie, when you walked in and found Andrea and me lounging in those big leather chairs you have in the library of your Presidential Suite, I had no idea what to expect. You'd never met us before and there we were, hanging out in your most expensive room, despite booking and paying for one of your least expensive rooms.

I'd like to tell you it was an accident or some sort of confusion, but it was neither. We were being nosy, looking around, and we stumbled upon the library. I only intended to sit down for a few seconds, but the chairs were so ridiculously comfortable and rather conducive for good conversation. You came in about ten minutes later.

We'd never done anything like that before, but I can't say I regret it, especially considering the events that followed. It was such a pleasure talking with you, Billie, and hearing all about your family. When you spoke about your son and daughter in particular, you had a sort of sparkle in your eyes and you smiled as you talked. Your love for them and pride in their accomplishments was easy to see.

It made me think of how proud I am of my own children and the joy I take in sharing their exploits and accomplishments. It's the nature of being a parent, along with the intrinsic empathy that comes with the role. We stand on the sidelines and cheer them on in the happy times and we hold their hands, feeling our own hearts break whenever they're hurting. When they're scared, we comfort them as best we're able, trying to protect them from all the monsters in the world.

It's not always an easy job and really, not a job at all. Being a parent is more like a great privilege, combined with a huge responsibility. I tell my kids all the time that as much as I worry about making the right decisions for the lives they're leading today, I also need to focus on the adults they will be in the future. What they want is not always what's best. It's up to Andrea and me to give them a solid foundation so they can move on to lead happy, healthy, and productive lives.

Just like with a healthy marriage, I believe love is the cornerstone of a healthy parent-child relationship. Our children need to know that no matter where they go in life or what they do, we will always love and accept them. Love should never be something a child needs to earn from their parent and it was nice to hear you agree with that, considering the successful, happy lives your own children have created for themselves.

When I met Andrea, she had two children from a prior relationship, a seven-year old son, Alexander, and a four-year-old daughter, Elizabeth. I loved those children as my own, right from the start, and we made sure to include them in our wedding ceremony. Both Alex and Liz got their own special rings and our first step as a family was making a joint commitment to each other before God.

Like any other blended family, we've had our challenges, but I've been there for those children and raised them as my own. It's been an incredible pleasure to watch them grow up and set their own courses in the world. Alex is in the Air Force now and Liz is about to be a senior in high school. The time has gone by so fast and my only disappointment is that I never had the opportunity to know them as babies.

Speaking of babies, how about the timing of Andrea's cousin giving birth? That baby being born on Andrea's birthday meant the world to her and she hasn't stopped going on about her "Birthday Buddy." It was a big surprise for everybody, because the baby came three weeks early. Though we're done having children and our youngest is three and a half years old, the birth seems to have triggered a sort of baby fever in Andrea

Her one regret about our trip was that she couldn't visit them in the hospital, since we were two hours away at Trakehner Inn. She was aching to hold a baby, something I didn't see on your list of amenities for the B&B. Yet, you still managed to provide the very best in service and you gave Andrea a baby to hold on her newly-shared birthday!

The arrival of your nine-week-old grandson was pure serendipity and just another sign to me that we were meant to be right where we were. It's wonderful how the Lord does that, giving little nudges along the way to let you know you're on the right path. Our visit to Trakehner Inn was full of them, indicators both small and large, letting us know we were supposed to be there.

Your grandson's long, brown hair reminded me of the birth of Andrea's and my first child together, our daughter, Kateri. She was also born with a full head of hair. That was an amazing experience, one of the greatest days of my life.

For weeks leading up to her birth, I heard all kinds of horror stories from friends and family, each of whom seemed sure I was going to pass out in the delivery room. I did my best to disregard their rousing vote of confidence in my ability to stay conscious and read as much as I could about the whole process.

Andrea had already been through it twice, with Alex and Liz, so she knew what to expect. At the same time, she wanted to do things differently with our children. She found a midwife in the area, Loraine, and chose to have her oversee the prenatal visits and then the birth. Andrea explained her reasons and I agreed that Loraine was a great choice. My only condition was that we do the birth in a hospital, just in case anything went wrong.

I did my best to be there for my wife throughout the pregnancy, catering to the unusual food requests, taking on a more involved role with my stepchildren, and being as supportive as I could. My medical conditions made things difficult at times, but I really tried my hardest to keep that away from Andrea, who already had more than enough on her plate.

When the day came, Andrea let me know we should go to the midwife's office and I sprang into action. I ran around the house and yes, I could still run in those days. I grabbed her bag, snacks for her in the hospital, and every conceivable thing we could possibly need. Then, I helped her into the car and raced to see the midwife.

We arrived at her office and I must have circled Andrea two or three times as we walked from the car to the front door. I was worrying about all things I might have forgotten at home, items we could need from the car, making sure my wife was ok to walk, and more. I was driving her absolutely crazy.

"This was it!" I thought. This was the day I had been waiting for and I could feel the excitement building up inside of me! I was about to become a daddy!

Once we got in that office, I was a frenetic mess, impatient beyond belief. Waiting for the midwife to examine Andrea and tell us to rush to the hospital felt like slow torture. Loraine went through the different steps of her examination, and right when I felt like I was about to explode in anticipation, she looked at me and suggested I take my wife out for a nice lunch. The baby wasn't ready yet.

If Loraine had turned and slapped me in the face, I don't think I would have been more surprised. I was so sure this was it and yet, the midwife, who just had her hands all over Andrea's business and seemed to know what she was talking about, told me to go have lunch. Never in my life have I been so disappointed to have someone tell me to eat something.

We headed to the nearby Olive Garden and I sat there feeling defeated, eating my chicken and gnocchi soup with breadsticks. There was still excitement in the air, because despite the midwife's relaxed demeanor, she did mention we were close. Andrea was positive that by the end of the day, we'd have our child.

Still, from a dad's perspective on the outside looking in, I didn't know what to think. I drowned my sorrows in a few bowls of soup and then asked to take more home in a to go container. Don't judge me, it's good soup.

In the end, Andrea proved right and Kateri really was born that night. Everything went according to plan and my wife was amazing. She didn't use an epidural and instead, relied on a self-hypnosis technique the midwife had introduced her to a few weeks earlier.

My mother and Liz were in the room and prior to her birth, we had no idea whether she'd be a girl or a boy. My stepdaughter, who was seven-years-old at the time, had the honor of seeing the baby first and announcing the gender to everyone else in the room.

I remember every detail of that birth, which is likely due to my anxiety disorders and PTSD. In stressful situations, I am in full control and my mind is sharp as a tack. I can't remember where I left my glasses or what I ate for breakfast on a normal day, but under pressure for short burst of time, I always rise to the occasion.

We were just getting Andrea into a special tub the hospital had for birthing mothers, when the baby made it known the time had come. Loraine recognized the signs and we immediately transferred Andrea to a wheelchair, then trucked her back to the room and helped her onto the bed.

Throughout the birth, I sat by Andrea's side and held her hand, while she did her thing. Andrea went into a zone and within a few minutes, I watched the miracle of life, right before my eyes. It was the most awe-inspiring and humbling experience of my life.

"It's a... It's a... I don't know!" shouted Liz.
"Come on!!! Is it a girl or a boy?" I yelled with baited anticipation.
[some indistinct chatter from the midwife and my mom]
"It's a girl!" exclaimed the proud, big sister.

That was the greatest moment of my life and I cried tears of pure joy, watching my wife nurse Kateri for the first time, then holding her myself, looking at the most incredible little bundle of possibilities. My mind raced with many different thoughts and emotions, but it kept coming back to "Thank you, Jesus! Thank you, thank you, thank you..."

The Lord blessed me with the honor of becoming a daddy twice more in the coming years, and each of their births were special in their own way. The midwife wasn't available for either one, but we made sure Andrea's doctors knew her birthing plan and allowed her the freedom to do things her way.

By the time my son, Joseph, was born, my medical limitations had increased to the point that I was able to drive Andrea to the hospital, but afterwards, my father-in-law had to drive me home. Even so, it was a great experience and we knew the baby was going to be a boy prior to his birth, so I was ecstatic at the notion that I would have both a daughter and a son.

Just like with Kateri's birth, I remember every little detail, but one memory always sticks out in my mind whenever I think of that day. I go back to the first moment I held my sweet little boy. I felt goose bumps all over my arms and a shiver go up my spine, as I looked at my newborn son and imagined what my dad must have felt when he first held me.

Our youngest daughter, Angelica, was born about four years later, and again, my limitations had grown worse with the time. I was no longer able to drive by that point, so a good friend of ours took Andrea and me to the hospital when the time came.

Once we got there, we sat in a small reception area, waiting for a room to be available. Imagine our surprise when we looked across the room and saw Loraine, the midwife who delivered Kateri. She was there with one of her clients and wasn't available to participate in the birth, but it was a wonderful sign from God that we were meant to be there. My worries were assuaged by a strong feeling that this last birth would be a good experience.

Compounding on the nostalgia, the nurse took Andrea's vitals and did a quick checkup, before leading us to the same delivery room where Kateri had been born. It was another sign from the big guy upstairs and it meant a whole lot to that anxious big guy in the delivery room.

We decided to play gender roulette again, since we already had one of each sex. Andrea and I figured we would be happy with whichever God chose to send us. In hindsight, the foreshadowing should have given me a clue that I was about to become the daddy of another little girl.

Angelica is three and a half years old as I write this, but she was her own person, right from the beginning. Watching her birth was surreal and comical, because she pulled a rock star entrance. Andrea went through the different labor steps until it was time to push and when she did, a brown balloon came out instead of a baby.

There was a brief silence, before the doctor laughed and I tried to explain to Andrea what I was seeing. She thought I was nuts, but thankfully, the doctor backed me up. He explained that it was the amniotic sac filled with fluid and it had somehow been delivered intact, though the baby was not in it.

He used a little stick to poke it and, in the process, forever ruined water balloons for me. Within a few seconds, Andrea felt a sudden urge to push and poof, my little Angel was born. "Angelica" was my idea, because I had already taken to calling Kateri my Princess and I wanted our new baby to have his or her own special pet name.

Joseph's nickname is "Big Fudge" and for the life of me, I don't remember the origin of it. I imagine it had something to do with his affinity for candy from the Fudge Kitchen in Cape May. One thing I do recall, something I could never forget, is his choice of a nickname for me. He was two-years-old at the time and since he was Big Fudge, he thought I should be "Big Hot Dog."

I spit water on my laptop the first time he said it, but I let him keep it going for a year or so. I eventually stopped him, because I didn't want Joseph to be embarrassed when he was old enough to understand why that nickname so hilarious. Besides, whenever he yelled it in public, I got disgusted looks from strangers.

Like I said earlier, Billie, being a parent is truly a great blessing and a huge responsibility. I make mistakes all the time like any other parent, but I take a ton of pride in knowing that no matter what, my children will never question how I feel about them. From hearing you talk about your son and daughter, I know that the same can be said for them.

When we spoke that day in the library, I mentioned my special bedtime routine with the children, but I forgot to tell you what it was. Each night before bed, I sit my son and daughters down individually and ask about their day. We talk about anything special that happened and what they're looking forward to in the days to come. Then, I repeat the same three sentences.

*You are my daughter (or son).*
*You are smart, you are strong, and you are beautiful (or handsome).*
*And I will always love you.*

## Chapter 3

It's hard to imagine what life must have been like for you, Billie, growing up at the Trakehner Inn. The property is massive and the Tudor-styled mansion, adorned in white plaster and dark-stained wood, looks like something out of a fairy tale. I had seen the pictures on your website and stumbled upon the real estate listing with images from every angle, but the reality is breathtaking. I was speechless when I first walked through your front door.

Those who know me well can tell you how rare a phenomenon that is. I've always had something to say, no matter where I've gone or who I've met along the way. Going back to my childhood, I had a terrible habit of speaking without thinking and saying things that upset or hurt others, especially in the heat of an emotional moment.

It didn't matter that I'd instantly regret the words, after they were expelled from my mouth or that it's pained me to see other people hurting. The words came out of my mouth and from that point, there was nothing I could do but apologize. A bell can't be unrung and making matters worse, my younger years were filled with times I withheld those apologies out of selfish pride and a foolish fear of being vulnerable.

That's what I thought of, as I sunk into one of your high-backed, fancy leather chairs in the foyer. I caused people pain and made a nuisance of myself in school, all because I never knew when to shut up. I'm not sure what led me there, but as a thunderstorm raged on outside, I stared out the leaded glass windows and my mind began to wander.

I grew up in a 1970s era suburban neighborhood in a small, rural community about an hour north of Philadelphia. My best friend lived across the street and each morning before school we'd walk to the bus stop together, where we'd meet up with other friends from our neighborhood.

I was a class clown in school and loved to make people laugh. Rare was a day that went by without me cracking jokes. My teachers all probably wanted to strangle me, despite what they might say now. It seemed like half the class enjoyed my jokes, while the other half would have enjoyed taking a turn with the whole strangling thing.

Rather than tone myself down, I consistently tried to convert the kids who didn't like me. It never worked and if anything, I made things worse. I'm not sure why. There's nothing kids appreciate more than having someone they already don't like, constantly bothering them and cracking dumb jokes, occasionally at their expense.

In short, I tried too hard and never understood that some people just didn't want to be my friend. Instead of focusing on all the friends I did have and appreciating them for all they brought to my life, I directed my attention to the others, who wanted nothing to do with me. Over time, I pushed people away and despite living in a neighborhood surrounded by other kids, I ended up feeling a profound sense of loneliness.

I became the troublemaker at school, albeit significantly different than what would be considered a troublemaker by today's standards. I never started fights or did anything malicious to purposely hurt someone else, but I did talk constantly, and my behavior was disrespectful to teachers and other students. Some of those teachers didn't just harbor fantasies of hurting me, they actually did it.

I was 9 years old when I was humiliated and beaten in front of my entire 4th grade class by a man who had no business teaching young children, I'll call him "Mr. Pain." The expandable walls between our classrooms had been opened up for a special hobby day and we were all allowed to bring in our favorite things to show our classmates. It was supposed to be a fun event.

One girl, who sat a couple seats down from mine, brought in her collection of little horse figurines and set them up in a long row across her desk. Looking back, she must have had a strong love of horses like you did, Billie. I didn't mean her any harm and I thought the little plastic figurines were neat, but when someone dared me to knock them over like dominoes, I jumped at the chance to get a laugh.

Almost immediately after I did it, I realized how much of a mistake I had made. The girl became extremely upset and started yelling, which drew a lot of attention. I tried to apologize as I helped her pick them up, but before I could finish, I felt a hand grab me from behind.

Mr. Pain lifted me off the ground by the back of my collar and carried me out into the hallway. He said very little, other than to tell me I was to sit at a desk out there and do the schoolwork he handed me. He ended with a menacing comment and articulated his plan to paddle me in front of the other students at the end of the day.

My parents had spanked me before and I was no stranger to Dad's leather belt, but I'd never been hit by a teacher. I spent the rest of the morning and afternoon sitting in that hallway, obsessing over the threat he had made. At the appointed time, another student came out to get me and bring me into the room.

I walked through the door and passed two of my teachers, both of whom just looked right through me. All the other kids were arranged in a big oval and Mr. Pain stood in the middle, with his foot on the seat of a desk and a thick, heavy wooden paddle in his hand. He decided not only to paddle me, but to also humiliate me. The normally gruff teacher had a big smile on his face and was going on and on, telling the class how hard he was going to spank me.

Mr. Pain made me bend over the desk in front of everybody and proceeded to beat me with the paddle, mocking me with each brutal swing. His jokes and insults got all the other kids laughing and every time I felt the crushing blow of wood on my backside, the class erupted in cheers and merriment.

No matter how hard I tried not to, I cried from the pain and my tears only served to provide more fodder for him and evoke more laughter from the other children. He hit me nine times with that paddle, once for every year of my age, and I have never felt so little, so helpless in my entire life. I had nowhere to go and nobody was willing to step in to protect me. Some of the other teachers had left the room before he began and the ones who stayed, turned their heads away about halfway through.

By the end of the whole ordeal, I couldn't sit down without feeling intense pain and when I got home, I found my rear end was covered in giant purple bruises. I was afraid to tell my parents what happened because I thought they would be mad at me and spank me too. That's what Mr. Pain told me when he was done. He said he was doing me a favor by not telling Mom and Dad.

The second time a teacher put their hands on me was four years later, in 8<sup>th</sup> grade. I'll call him "Mr. Rage." It was a Friday afternoon and one of my teachers had split our class into small groups to play a trivia game. The problem began when he asked a question with his back to the class, as he was updating the scores on the board.

Someone from another team blurted out a silly answer and Mr. Rage snapped. He spun around with fire in his eyes and demanded to know who said it. Everyone in that class recognized that he was in a terrible mood, except one girl, who pointed at me and loudly proclaimed, "Ben Miller said it."

There was a look of shock on the other students and nobody else dared to utter a word. She told me later that someone at her table made the comment, but she thought it would be funny to say I did. That girl had no idea what she started.

Mr. Rage stormed over to me, glared into my eyes and said with a very odd, unnatural voice, "Get out. Sit by the door and don't move." I tried to protest that I hadn't said anything and he gave me a look that told me all I needed to know. I got up and left the room without another word.

When the bell rang for the end of class, I tried to leave and Mr. Rage grabbed my shirt in a clenched fist. He yanked me into the classroom and snarled, "You're not going anywhere!" I had no idea what to expect and I'm not ashamed to tell you I was terrified. He waited until all the other students left the room and then he closed the door behind them.

Mr. Rage walked over to me and began, "You really think you're something, don't you? You're big sh*t?" I tried again to tell him I hadn't said anything, but he cut me off by roaring, "Shut the f*ck up! Your time to talk is over and now it's my turn!"

Both the language and his tone caught me by surprise and fear sharply rose inside of my brain. He grabbed the collars of my shirt and slammed me into the wall, looking square into my eyes, saying, "If you open your f*cking mouth one more time, I'm gonna kick the sh*t out of you, right here and right now!"

The fear had turned to pure terror by that point and I didn't say another word. He, on the other hand, had much more to say. "You know why people don't like you? Because you're an a**hole! The other teachers don't like you, the students don't like you. You're a cocky little a**hole that nobody can stand and I'm sick of your bullsh*t!"

Then he took it the next level, "You know I'm one of the [local sports team] coaches, right?"

I didn't answer.

"Well I am and if you open your f*cking mouth one more time in my class, I'm gonna have a little talk with them. I'm gonna have them come beat the sh*t out of you and shut you up for good! Then you won't say another God d*mn word, will you? What do you have to say about that? Not so f*cking cocky anymore, are you? Are we clear?"

I was shaking so badly by that point that even if I wanted to say something, I don't think I would have been able. It was all compounded by the verity that I'd done nothing wrong that day and I had no idea why he was so angry with me.

The confrontation ended with him saying these words to me, "You better keep your mouth shut about our conversation here, because I'll deny everything. Nobody's gonna take your word over mine. You're a cocky little piece of sh*t and I'm a teacher. Now get the f*ck out of here and don't forget what I said."

Believe me, Billie, when I say that he didn't need to add that last part. I've never forgotten it and I kept that secret for over 25 years, until I told my wife. I never said a word to my parents, my friends or anyone else. At the time, I believed he was right that nobody would take my word over his. Truth is, I believed everything he said to me and that day changed the way I looked at myself for many years. I still have lingering doubts that were born in his angry tirade

Three decades later, sitting in that supple leather chair, watching the thunder clouds rolling in over the Pocono mountains, I don't understand what led my mind to that solitary chapter in my life. I'm an adult now, a husband and parent to five children and stepchildren. My oldest kid fixes planes for the United States Air Force and I'm a disabled veteran myself.

Still, as Andrea took what she said was a much-needed nap in our bed upstairs, that's what I thought about while I gazed over your rolling lawns and listened to the rain drops tapping on the glass. She walked downstairs as the storm was concluding and hearing Andrea's voice helped bury the ghosts of my past once again.

## Chapter 4

It seems the weather can be rather dramatic in the mountains and change at a moment's notice. The sun came out while the rain was still falling and by the time it was done, the dark sky had given way to a pale blue. Walking outside onto the veranda felt like stepping into an oil painting. It's easy to see why the Poconos are often called "God's country."

I also noticed that the sun, which had been obscured by the storm clouds a few minutes earlier, suddenly felt pretty darn hot. You must have a switch inside or near the house for the fountains in the pool, because they had been turned on, but I never saw you out there. The pool fountains were shooting up into the air, creating little rainbows on the stone and mortar pool deck.

Andrea isn't a big pool person, though she'll go in with the kids or to feel refreshed on a hot day. She much prefers laying in the sun and reading. I, on the other hand, am happy to float the day away or sit half submerged on a pool ledge for hours at a time.

I've never really thought about it before, but my wife's and my pool preferences are similar to those of my parents, just in reverse. Dad did not enjoy pools and Mom loved them. We never had one growing up, but after my brother, sister, and I were older and moved out, they decided to put in a gorgeous inground pool in our backyard. While Dad hated swimming, he lived to make Mom happy and spent innumerable hours keeping that pool in pristine condition for her.

They figured that with their kids out of the house, the pool would be a quiet oasis for Mom and her friends. One thing they didn't count on was their youngest son, who was serving overseas in the Navy, unexpectedly coming home a disabled veteran. Surprise. That was one of the most difficult times in my life, but my parents were very good to me and helped make a tough transition a little bit easier. Also, I had their pool to float around in, when Mom wasn't out there with her old lady friends.

She'd surely smack me if she was here to read that last sentence, but she's over at her house, well beyond smacking distance. Even so, there's a part of me that flinched when I wrote it. I've been on the end of mom's and Dad's wrath more than a few times in my life, and I earned every single bit of it. Like I said before, I wasn't a bad kid who tried to hurt other people, but I had a smart mouth and a wicked sense of humor that wasn't everyone's cup of tea.

I also made plenty of normal teenager mistakes, like being a general annoyance to my neighbors, missing curfew, and getting a speeding ticket in my parents' car. That police officer followed me all the way home and pulled me over in my own driveway. Luckily for me, Mom was outside on the patio and heard the whole thing. That made it so much easier when it came time for my parents to lecture and discipline me.

See what I mean about earning those punishments? I could go on and on about the multitude of stupid things I did that caused my parents grief, like smashing a pumpkin on Halloween to impress my friends, lighting off fireworks at all hours of the night, prank calls in the humble days before caller id… You get the point.

Despite my never-ending shenanigans, I never had to question if they loved me or supported me. They may not have supported some of the decisions I made, but they always supported me as a person. Mom and Dad weren't perfect, just as Andrea and I surely aren't, but they did the best they could with what they had.

Mom was a physical education teacher, though she became a homemaker, due to a combination of medical conditions and her desire to be home with her children when we were young. Dad was also a teacher, dual-certified in secondary English and History. He taught at our local high school for 38 years before he retired.

I grew up in the 70s and 80s, at a time when teachers weren't making anywhere near what they deserved. To support our family, Dad worked at a local market after school, performed magic shows at special events, played saxophone in a local band, and sold men's clothing at a store in the mall.

The magic and saxophone were mostly before I was born and during my early years, though he practiced both throughout my childhood and having a father who knew magic was pretty great. I probably had enough coins pulled out of my nose and ears to buy a small cottage in Nantucket. He also played the piano and several other instruments, self-taught on each of them.

While Dad's passion was music, Mom loved her sports. She coached field hockey, volleyball, basketball, and softball. My sister played basketball on my mom's team and the mere mention of it requires me to tell you a story that's become legend in our family.

Dad had taken me to see one of her games on a rare day off for him. We walked into the old Junior High School gym, waved to Mom and sister, then headed up into the bleachers. Somewhere in the middle, there was an accident, which caused my sister to fall and broke a bone. I want to say it was her arm, but I was young and that detail eludes me.

What I do remember was Mom yelling from the bench, "Get up, you're fine!" as Dad bolted down the bleachers and out onto the court. He later explained that he could hear the "crack" from our seat. Boy, did Mom ever feel bad about that one. My sister could do no wrong for weeks afterwards.

In fairness, Dad once caught part of my brother's finger in a door and the end of it was accidentally chopped off. They wrapped his hand in a towel and put the piece of finger on ice, then rushed my brother to the ER. The surgeon did an unbelievable job at reattaching it and today, he has full use of his finger and you can't even see a scar.

Guess I lucked out on the old parental injury spectrum, though I did once catch a football with my left eye. I also busted my head open by sledding down our staircase on a pillow and slamming into the flagstone hallway at the bottom. Both times, I got Dad's patented emergency plan- a dishrag to apply pressure, a baggie filled with ice, and a quick trip to the ER. Between my brother, sister, and me, they knew us well at that hospital and probably kept an extra stitching kit handy.

Once I reached about 7th grade, Dad was working constantly, spending days at the school, then nights and weekends at that clothing store. He rarely got any days off and when he did, he spent it with us. His one guilty pleasure was reading, a hobby he and Mom shared. They both had long reserve lists at our local library. Mom was happy to read in her recliner or up in bed, while Dad preferred to read outside.

He loved nature and our backyard was filled with maple trees Dad had planted when they built the house. He would lay out there reading in the shade for hours, taking occasional breaks to watch the birds or squirrels and pet his beloved cat, Pumpkin. I think I was about 10 years old when Pumpkin passed away and that was a very sad day for us all.

Mom was more of a dog person and she especially loved Saint Bernards. I grew up with those giant slobber machines and I consider myself lucky for the experience. Mom bought those dogs so many toys and treats it was ridiculous. Truth is, both my parents spoiled the dogs rotten.

I can't tell you how many mornings I would come down before school to see Dad at the kitchen table, holding his coffee mug with one hand and petting the dog with the other. When the dog was sufficiently satisfied that all her itches were addressed, she would lay down and he would go back to grading papers.

Reminders of my parents were all around me as I descended into the Trakehner Inn pool and it was impossible not to think of them. Mom loved the kind of chairs you had on the pool deck and just two weeks earlier, she told me she planned on buying one. Dad, ever the nature guy, wouldn't have cared less about the chairs, but would have loved the flowering bushes that surrounded the pool and all the animals they attracted.

That water was cold, too, probably because of all the rain. With the way the sun had heated things up after the storm, it felt great once I had acclimated to it. The water temperature would have been perfect for my mom. She didn't enjoy pool water that was either too cold, like in the 60s, or too warm, like in the mid to high 80s.

"Refreshing" is the way she always described her perfect pool experience. "Dry and out of the pool" is the way Dad always described his perfect pool experience. Quite a pair, those two…

Dad retired from teaching in 1998, and it took about two weeks before he started going out of his mind with boredom. He had been working non-stop since he was a boy and he told me he needed something to feel like he was still being a productive citizen.

Dad began volunteering at the library, at a radio reading service for the blind, and at our local visitor's center. I also volunteered there for years, prior to technological advances and dwindling listenership forcing them to close their doors. It was a radio station that broadcast programming specifically targeted to those who were vision impaired.

Each day, volunteers would read the local newspapers, advertisements for area grocery stores, national and international news would be broadcast, as well as programming for children. Subscribers to the station were given special receivers that were able to pick up the broadcasts, at no cost to them. Dad read grocery store ads and I was an engineer/producer. I followed his lead and we were both members of the Board of Directors.

My father was the greatest man I've ever known, and he devoted his life to giving back to others, right up until the night he died, March 1st, 2004. I was at home that evening, playing on my computer, when Mom called me to tell me something was wrong with Dad.

She called twice, and I missed both calls, but she left a quick message the second time, telling me something had happened with Dad. As soon as I heard it, I immediately called her back and learned he had fallen down in the house and the ambulance was there. That's as much as she got out before I told her I was coming and hung up.

I lived about three miles away and drove a Mustang, which I pushed to the limit on that mad dash to the home where I had grown up. In the brief trip, my mind raced and I thought about talking to him earlier in the day. He had a cold and said he didn't feel well, but he sounded ok other than that. I was thoroughly unprepared for what I found when I got to the house.

Our family home was on a corner lot and it was surrounded by a couple police cars, two ambulances, and all kinds of other vehicles with flashing lights. I'm sure the response was due to my brother being a local police officer and Dad having such a strong presence in our small community. They had all come out to help.

I parked as close as I could to the house and ran for the open front door. Once I got inside, I found Mom in the living room crying and she told me he was upstairs. I took those steps two at a time and met a big crowd of people in the upstairs hallway. To my right, I saw my brother pacing in my parent's bedroom. All he could say was, "It's not good, Ben. It's not good."

I had to fight the strong urge to push past those people in the hall and get to Dad, because I knew they were there to help and there was nothing I could do. Instead, I went downstairs to comfort my mom. Only a few minutes passed, and I heard them moving across the upstairs hallway to the steps. Mom and I rushed out into the foyer in time to see them bringing Dad down the stairs on a stretcher.

His eyes were open and it looked as if his arm had moved, but I later learned it just slid off the stretcher. Still, I was holding out hope that he would be ok. Then, they reached the bottom of the stairs and everything changed. While I was looking for signs of life and an indication of what had happened, I heard the paramedic speak two words that have haunted me ever since, "Resume CPR."

I had ridden as an attendant with our local ambulance squad years earlier and while I was in college, I was certified as a Red Cross First Aid and CPR Instructor. I knew what those words meant.

CPR is only used as a last resort outside of a hospital, because even under ideal circumstances, with the patient being treated immediately by someone with proper training, the chance of survival is only about 10%. If there is a delay in treatment, like having to wait for the ambulance, that number drops to 4%. That's why the first thing a paramedic will try is the defibrillator, which has about a 40% chance of survival. If it's unsuccessful, they'll move to CPR. Once it's started, they're required by law to continue until a doctor declares the patient dead.

Despite what I knew and what I'm sure my brother knew, we both kept our mouths shut and I drove Mom to the hospital. Mom and I beat the ambulance there and while she was in the waiting room, I met them at the ER loading dock.

When the doors opened, I saw Dad's eyes were closed. I slowly nodded at the medic, who I had known for years and he looked down as they walked past me. I headed inside to wait with my mom. Several doctors tried again to resuscitate Dad in the ER, but he was gone. It was a sudden myocardial infarction, a heart attack.

That was the worst day of my life. Dad was my best friend and he died seeing me swimming in a sea of failure. I was all alone, grossly overweight, unemployed, and struggling to stay sober, as I battled with disabilities I had yet to acknowledge.

Dad would have been so happy to meet my wife and children, to read my magazine columns and books, and to watch me on TV. It would have pained him to see how hard I struggle and how much of my life I've lost to my medical conditions, but he would have been especially proud of the philanthropic campaigns I've created. I may not be able to work anymore, but I still try to find ways to follow in his footsteps and remain a productive citizen.

It was hard not to think Dad while I was swimming in the pool. I imagined him vacuuming it for Mom to make sure the water was perfect or relaxing in a chair by one of the flowering bushes, reading a book as Mom swam. I miss him so much, Billie.

## Chapter 5

I've stayed at hotels and B&Bs all over the country, but I've never known a place like Trakehner Inn. That historic old home, constructed as a retreat for the builder's family and his friends in society's elite, seemed to be imbued with a spiritual energy more powerful than anything I'd encountered before. Having spent your entire life there, I figure you're intimately familiar with the divine, reflective force that fills the air and permeates the walls.

Some might suggest those who came before us and have since left our Earthly realm are still wandering the halls of Trakehner Inn, and after what I experienced, I'm not so sure I'd disagree. Did I unknowingly interact with one of the former Presidents who vacationed here, or maybe a beloved family member who's no longer with us? There's no way to be certain and frankly, there were more than a few times when I felt like God almighty was sitting next to me, because the peace and love I experienced were more profound than I had ever known or could adequately express in words.

That first day was therapeutic, but overwhelming, as I relived some of the most difficult chapters in my life. Meanwhile, Andrea was having one of the more restful and relaxing vacations she'd experienced in years. Any trip with no kids repeatedly calling out "Mommy" is a plus, but the energy at Trakehner Inn and the restorative effects of the woods were welcome salves to heal her frazzled nerves. We decided to take it easy on our first night and stay in, having pizza delivered and watching "Grey's Anatomy" on Netflix.

My friends like to make fun of me for watching it, but I enjoy the show and all the powerful characters it features. Meredith Grey has been killed four or five times, yet she always seems to come back stronger and more focused. My favorite is Richard Webber, who'd known deep sorrow and faced more challenges than anyone ever should, yet he's always managed to keep his composure, his sense of humor, and make the right choices to ensure his dignity remains intact. I know he's not a real person, but I admire the character nonetheless.

So, there we were, large bacon pizza positioned on the luggage rack, towels spread over the bed sheets to prevent us from making a mess and ruining them. I flipped the program on and settled into bed next to Andrea. The pizza was loaded with bacon and delicious. The show was as compelling as always, and I was able to tune out and relax. Everything was going well until the second episode we watched, which revolved around a young boy with a brain tumor.

I've never known anyone with a brain tumor, but I did know a little boy who was taken from his family way too early. That boy was my friend and he was 8 years old when he was hit by a car and killed in front of my house. I was six years old, but despite my early age, there's little that I don't remember about that day.

We all lived in that same suburban neighborhood I mentioned before and us kids were a tight group. We rode bikes together, played all kinds of games with each other, made forts in the neighboring corn fields; it was an idyllic childhood. Sure, we had our occasional fights and disagreements like any other kids, but there was never anything serious.

It was a late spring day in 1981, sunny and beautiful. A group of kids got together to play ball on an empty lot we called "the hole," and I was riding my bike around the neighborhood to see who else was around. Everything was quiet until suddenly, it wasn't.

Out of nowhere, my best friend's father drove up to me and frantically asked if I was with his son. I told him I wasn't and he asked if I knew where he son was. Again, I told him no.

Without a word, he sped off around the corner. Something seemed wrong, so I turned around and rode my bike home. When I got there, I saw many flashing lights, police officers walking around in front of my house, and nervous parents milling about. My own parents were outside and grabbed me into a hug as soon as they saw me. That's when I noticed Mom was crying.

I asked what was wrong and nobody would say anything, so I scurried up the tree I often climbed in my front yard. From that vantage point, I could see the police cars, an ambulance, and a fire truck. They were all down by the highway about a block in front of my house. I noticed a lone shoe lying in the road.

As I surveyed the scene, I watched two police officers walk over to the parents, who had come together into a big group on the corner of my front lawn. I don't know what the officers said, but wails of sadness and grief emanated from the parents.

It was horrible and I knew everyone was hurting, but I had no idea what had happened. From up in that tree, I watched a police officer walk with one of the adults from our neighborhood and take her into the house across the street. Then, I saw another officer walk my friend's family into my house. That's when I climbed down and went inside to find out what had happened.

There was chaos inside and a palpable feeling of what I can now describe as anguish. Mom and Dad did their best to keep themselves together for my friend's parents and older brother, who were dealing with a pain my young mind couldn't possibly grasp. My parents waved me away, so I went back outside and listened to some of the other adults, who were still talking on my lawn.

One of them said that my friend was with a group playing ball and when the ball went into the road, he ran after it without thinking. A different neighbor said something about him running after other kids who had crossed the road. I still don't know exactly what happened, other than he had made a mistake we all made at some point in our young lives, never appreciating the inherent danger.

It was terrible luck that this time, he just happened to run out in front of a car. The driver of that car was the neighbor I saw go into the house across the street and from what the police said, it all happened too fast for her to stop.

I didn't know how to feel so I began crying, so I climbed back up into the place I felt safest: my tree. When the streets were cleared of flashing lights and grieving adults, I carefully lowered myself into the soft grass, snuck into the house as quietly as I was able, and hid in my bedroom until my parents found me later that night. They tried to explain what had happened, but I was too young to truly understand the awful loss our community had just suffered.

Two years later, I learned more lessons in loss, when my beloved great-grandfather died. I called him "Pappy" and he gave me a quarter every time I saw him. I was eight years old at the time and though he was 81, his death was a sudden and a painful blow to my family. Pappy was the kind of guy everybody liked. He was one of the nicest men you could ever hope to meet and he never hesitated to lend a hand where he was able. He was also tough as nails.

One time, in his 70s, he was up on a neighbor's roof fixing something, when he slipped and fell off. The neighbors rushed to his aid and by the time they got there, Pappy stood up, said he was ok, then added, "Don't tell Reba." Reba was my great-grandmother. Though a loving woman, she didn't quite have Pappy's temperament or patience.

Losing him was very confusing to me and I'd have dreams where he was still alive and we'd talk. I tried to understand what it meant to die, but it didn't make sense that God took both the old and young, with no reason and no notice. Pappy's funeral was the first one I attended and it was important to my parents that we were all there, but it only confused me more.

I a stranger lying in the casket, not the Pappy I knew and loved. His face looked different and he wasn't wearing his glasses, because my great-grandmother had accidentally scratched them. I wasn't afraid to be in that room, but I grew more and more confused as the funeral progressed.

After Pappy came the deaths of several more relatives who were older and while I could appreciate death as a natural part of life, it never got any easier for me to accept. I joined my local volunteer fire department and rescue squad as soon as I was old enough and although we helped a lot of people, we also worked the scenes of more than a few deaths. Despite not knowing any of them personally, each of their deaths acutely affected me.

My mid to late teen years saw me waiting around fatal car accidents for the coroner to arrive, scanning the horizon at a local quarry for drowning victims, and trying to console a man who had accidently run over a friend and coworker with a bulldozer. They were all tragic and painful in their own way, and there are certain areas of my hometown I can't go past without reliving those bad memories in my head.

Then, I compounded my issues with death by inadvertently pursuing a job that would put me right in the middle of it. I graduated with honors from my training in Naval Intelligence and as part of the reward for the high marks, I got to pick my first duty station from a list of available orders.

I chose an air reconnaissance squadron in Spain that was operating as part of America's NATO contingent during the

Bosnian War. My job was to monitor and track people who were killing each other, making notes about the weapons they used to do it. I was cleared Top Secret, with access to sensitive compartmented information, keyhole satellite intel, and specific aspects of communications intelligence.

What happened over there was horrific, barbaric, and one of the worst atrocities our world has seen since the holocaust. Ethnic cleansing and the torture of innocent people were routine, with entire families murdered and thrown into mass graves. There seemed to be no dignity or respect for human life.

I monitored more than a few active missile systems, along with planes that didn't belong in the air, under the no-fly zone we were enforcing. Things went to the next level just before Thanksgiving in 1994, when Serbian soldiers tried to bring down one of our intel planes with a surface to air missile.

The nature of my job precludes me from sharing more of this story, but I can tell you they were not successful and the response from NATO involved a series of bombing runs that ensured they would no longer have the capability to do it again.

I worked with a very specific piece of equipment that is probably outdated today but was in its developmental stage at the time. It helped me tell elaborate stories about where different pieces of military hardware were located with absolute precision, and because of that, I was tasked with providing target intel for those bombings runs.

The Navy never officially told me so, but a lot of people died, in part, because I did my job. I read the Sitrep (a report generated each day to detail the previous day's activities on both sides and current conditions) after the bombings and it clearly noted where they had taken place, along with belligerent casualty numbers. It wasn't hard to put everything together and once I did, I was never the same again.

My complicated relationship with death had taken a new twist and it was something I was not equipped to handle. I began having what I would later learn were panic attacks, but at the time, felt like a series of nervous breakdowns. Back in the mid-1990s, nobody knew about panic attacks and there was no internet to look things up. I thought I was going crazy. My Navy career ended that day, though I remained in uniform a few more months before I was given my honorable discharge and sent home.

Not long after I came home, I lost another friend in a drunk driving accident. Then, a year later, a teammate of mine from our high school soccer team was killed in a tragic series of events at college.

In the years that followed, I lost a good friend and former coworker to suicide, one of the nicest and most kind-hearted friends I've ever had died from a sudden heart attack, another old friend was killed in a horrendous accident at work, a childhood friend from my old neighborhood took his own life in his parent's basement, and the depressing list of sadness keeps going. Just last month, I stood in front of the casket of one more longtime friend.

I've seen many deaths on Grey's Anatomy, but they rarely look and feel like death in real life. When Grandpa had a sudden heart attack, six months after Dad, it happened in the hospital after a minor surgery and doctors were able to resuscitate him. He lived about 15 hours after that, long enough for all of us to say our goodbyes, something we never got with Dad. As much as we appreciated that time, it wasn't enough. I imagine it's never enough when you're losing someone you love.

I held Grandpa's hand as he passed away, with my uncle holding his other hand, and family gathered in the room. Of all the deaths I've witnessed, and there's been way too many, his was the most peaceful. He was unconscious at the time and slowly drifted away.

Grandpa was a great man who touched many lives and along with Dad, he taught me what it meant to be a husband and father. I'm deeply grateful that God blessed me with the two of them and as much as I miss them both, I try each day to carry on their legacy by being the man they always hoped I would become. I hope I haven't disappointed them.

# Chapter 6

The hour was nearing midnight when we turned off the TV.
I looked over at the luggage stand and laughed, thinking
that we were probably the first guests in all of Trakehner
Inn's years as a B&B, who used it as a sideboard to serve
dinner. It occurred to me that if I filled the bathroom
garbage can with ice, it would make a lovely champagne
bucket. I kept that thought to myself, however, since I'm a
recovering alcoholic, Andrea doesn't drink, and we're not
hillbillies.

Every now and then, I like to give my wife some hope that
the guy she married isn't a complete nitwit. Trust me when
I say that I've given her plenty of reasons to question it.
Earlier that very day, I nearly knocked myself out walking
into the bathroom door, because I was looking out the
window.

At lunch, I threw a piece of cheese at Andrea in the hopes
that it would stick to her cheek. It was an attempt to make
her laugh, which she likely would have done, had we not
been in the middle of a crowded cafe, with the waitress
standing at our table.

Andrea told me I was an idiot and I said she was lucky I
hadn't thrown it at the waitress, who walked away at that
point. My comment led to her standard glare and slow head
shake. Then, I told her to put all the silverware in her purse,
finally garnering me the laugh I had been trying to achieve.
The whole whispered "put this in your purse" joke started
on our first date.

We were at the steakhouse I mentioned before and conversation flowed freely throughout the meal. Afterwards, things got a little awkward and quiet, so I improvised. I picked up the bottle of steak sauce, looked at her with as serious a face as I could muster, then leaned over the table and whispered, "Here, put this in your purse."

Her response was priceless. It began as a look of befuddled shock, then when I cracked a smiled, she burst out in the most melodious laughter and her face turned bright red. It was exactly like that day in the call center, when she talked to the teacher who wanted to drug up all her students and drag them on a whale watching trip.

Bright red cheeks, tears flowing down her face, with her head in her hands and loud laughter disturbing everyone around us… I knew right then and there that she was the one.

From that day forward, our relationship has been a never-ending skirmish for control. I have constantly tried to find new ways to make her laugh and she has repeatedly tried to make me understand that I'm a 43-year-old father of five. My wife thinks loudly talking about an imaginary crystal meth addiction in public places is inappropriate. I did that at the cafe too and despite what she might tell you, Andrea did laugh.

Thing is, Billie, my life is not fun and carefree like I portray it to others. I spend a good deal of the typical day, isolated and alone. It began after I came home from the military and has gotten progressively worse with each passing year. My official psychiatric diagnosis is Panic Disorder with Agoraphobia, Generalized Anxiety Disorder, Post Traumatic Stress Disorder, and Depression. Oh yeah, can't forget to add binge eating disorder to that mélange of madness.

I'm grateful to the Department of Veterans Affairs (VA), as imperfect as the organization may be, for all that they've done for me and helped me do for my family. When I was no longer able to work, by the beginning of 2008, the VA increased my disability level to 100% and made it possible for me to still provide for my wife and children. The amount of my disability pay is far below what I made working in the business world, but it's plenty to make sure my family is fed, clothed, and given a roof over their heads.

Because I've learned tricks to hide my pain and put on a good show when I interact with other people, most have no idea how much I struggle every day. Simple things like leaving my home or carrying on a basic conversation, are exceedingly difficult for me. I get easily confused when I talk and end up repeating myself or restating something another person already said, because I don't remember. My house is my safe place and especially my bedroom, where I hide every night after 5pm, because being around people, even my family, gets way too overwhelming.

Things like writing, and the charitable work I've done in the past decade make me feel useful again and it's great to be able to help other people. At the same time, both are incredibly overwhelming. I can only do things in bursts and there's no consistency. One day, I'll be good to go for a few hours and the next, I just stare at my computer screen.

When I do write, I forget and rewrite the same paragraph multiple times, or I confuse the words. The first draft of this letter to you was embarrassing and I needed Andrea's help to sort it out.

I have never stopped attempting to get better. Along with trying all kinds of different medicines to find the right ones that help me more than their side effects hurt me, I see multiple doctors on a regular basis. Every three to four months, I visit a VA Psychiatrist to talk about my conditions and get refills of the medicines covered by the VA. I also go to a private psychiatrist every two months to have the same conversations and get refills of the medicines that the VA won't provide me. Additionally, each week, I meet with a private psychologist for 45 minutes of therapy.

Few people know exactly what I did overseas in the Navy, including most of those who worked at the squadron with me. In the intelligence community, "Need to Know" is a phrase that is strictly followed, both in and out of the workplace.

I worked with Fleet Air Reconnaissance Squadron Two, or "VQ-2" for short. The job that I did there was different than the one I had been taught to do at Corry Station, a Navy training facility that was later renamed The Center for Information Dominance and is now called The Center for Information Warfare.

My official designation was Cryptology Technician Technical (CTT), though people in other ratings typically just called us "Spooks." In today's Navy, the job title still exists, but it's much different than it once was. There was a merger with the former Electronic Warfare rating and undoubtedly, a lot of technological advances that I wouldn't know about.

My squadron was based out of an unassuming building, positioned next to the runway at the Naval Air Station in Rota, Spain. The CTT work space was in a secure area on the second floor of the building, protected by a remotely-opened steel cage, two solid steel doors with individual cipher locks, and a security detail. It carried the nondescript designation, "N6."

Not long after I arrived at the squadron, I was approached by one of my superiors about working on a special project. It involved a groundbreaking new technique of intelligence collection that would eventually make our traditional methods obsolete. Since my intention was to stay in the Navy for 20 years and retire, then pursue an intelligence job in the civilian sector, I jumped at the opportunity to start my career with a such a high-profile assignment.

I was asked to file a request to spend my entire initial enlistment period at VQ-2, which was quickly approved, and I was kept away from the office while I underwent specialized training. During that period, I worked as a clerk in the squadron's mail room, training either before or after my shift, depending on the day.

My training took about six months to bring me up to speed, and every few weeks, they'd come up with some new excuse why I had to stay in the mailroom. Other than the officer I spoke with and the representative from the equipment manufacturer who was training me, I have no idea who else knew what I was tasked to do.

Once I finally made it up to N6, I was ready to get to work and extremely eager to prove myself. I was brought right into the mix with our squadron's commitments to NATO operations Deny Flight, Provide Promise, and Sharp Guard. It wasn't an easy job and what I witnessed happening in the Balkans was a series of horrors no human being should ever have to endure.

I wasn't naïve and I understood what war entailed, but nothing prepared me for what I witnessed. No movie or tv show can ever properly portray the reality of man's ability to brutalize one another. People died every day and not just soldiers, but innocent civilians and children, who were no threat to anybody.

Those narratives portrayed in daily sitreps and the images we received were seared into my brain. I also had a very real fear that I would make a mistake and miss something that could lead to one of our planes being shot down or cost somebody their life. Then, one day, I was ordered to help do the latter.

Please understand, I am no combat veteran. I was never in a position where I was forced to kill another man to save my own life or the life of somebody else. I never fought on a battlefield to free a nation or help preserve basic human rights. My job was to watch the atrocities from above and provided intel from afar.

I handled it all ok at first. What was happening to the civilians bothered me, especially the children, but I continuously reminded myself that it was out of my hands. There was nothing I could do to change any of it, so I threw myself into my work and tried to prove how good I was. I looked at the combatants as colored circles on a screen, numbers on a sheet of paper, and when I targeted their locations around missile and radar sites, it never occurred to me that they were real people.

That's what I had been taught to do. Depersonalizing the enemy is the military's way of keeping emotions out of the equation, along with the liabilities that come with those emotions. I did everything I was supposed to do and I was good at my job to the point of being arrogant about my abilities.

Then one morning after a bombing run, I was reading a sitrep, and those numbers became people as real as I was, with families waiting for them, just like mine. Something changed inside, and it suddenly occurred to me that I played a part in many of their deaths. It's not as if I'm simple-minded and never realized what was happening before that point, but I was detached.

Aside from what I mentioned about depersonalizing the enemy, there's a significant difference between pulling a trigger on the front lines of a combat zone and doing what I did. It hadn't crossed my mind that by providing the locations of military equipment, manned and surrounded by people who were then killed, I would bear partial responsibility for their deaths.

I'd like to be able to say I was a strong guy who wasn't fazed by the sudden realization, but that's not what happened. It hit me like a ton of bricks and I broke down. I experienced a range of emotions that was unlike anything I had ever encountered before.

I would later learn that was my first panic attack. Until my dying breath, I will remember every detail of that moment, from where I was standing to the smell of the perfume on the female Petty Officer next to me. Afterwards, I composed myself and went back to work with a much different mindset and a whole lot of uncertainty over what had just happened.

I still did my job exactly as I was trained to do it, and I provided whatever was asked of me. I never stopped giving everything I had to give. We were on the right side of the conflict, of that I have always been sure, but some people aren't meant to have the responsibilities that came with my job, and it quickly became apparent that I was one of them

On top of my moral dilemma, I still didn't understand what has happening to me and worried I was going crazy, but there was nobody I could talk to about it. My only choice was our Intel Officer, but I was afraid to talk with her about my struggles and I was positive she didn't want to hear that I was having trouble doing what the Navy had spent so much time, money, and effort training me to do.

My only real confidant I trusted back then was alcohol and we became closer than I care to admit. It would help me through immeasurable pain over the coming years, then cause its own, which was much worse. Let me stop here, so I don't get ahead of myself.

## Chapter 7

Billie, I laid there in that bed for hours, while Andrea slept peacefully beside me, just like every other night. Old wounds never get a chance to completely heal, because I keep ripping the scabs off each night. I don't do it on purpose and I'd love nothing more than to simply close my eyes like she does and fall into a restful slumber. That doesn't seem to be an option for me.

I don't know what it is about Trakehner Inn, but everything was coming back to me with such intensity and no stone remained unturned, in my cerebral cemetery. I felt as if I were that young man again, feeling all my security and sense of identity being ripped away. Eventually, I carefully slipped out of bed and went downstairs.

I figured I would get some water from the water cooler, sit in the parlor for a little, and try to calm my mind. Instead, I began to grow even more introspective and I felt a strong urge to do the exact opposite of what I had come downstairs to do. Something inside of me was saying to quit letting fear cripple me and finally face my demons, once and for all.

It makes no Earthly sense why I would take advice like that, even if it did come from within, or at least feel as if it did. I've worked for years with my doctors, to attempt to put behind me what happened overseas and keep the panic and PTSD demons at bay. The last thing I wanted to do was purposely go back there, then poke the proverbial bear. Yet, for whatever reason, I gave in to that inner voice and did it anyway.

Sitting down in that big leather chair, I took myself back to my days in uniform and I tried to focus on the aftermath of that first attack. It didn't take long until I could feel myself right back there, experiencing those sensations of uncertainty and sadness. The latter took me by surprise, because I expected fear.

When I'm lying in bed at home and my mind goes back there in the darkness of night, the sense of fear is suffocating. Sitting in your oversized chair and looking at the same fireplace that once warmed Teddy Roosevelt, I didn't feel the slightest bit of fear. Instead, I remembered the sadness that hung over my head when this all started and how devastating it felt to lose everything that meant so much to me.

After my first attack overseas, back in the Navy, I struggled to keep pushing forward. Amid the confusion was hope that it was a one-time thing, which was quickly dashed when I had more attacks in the days that followed. My mind was going in all different directions and I did my best to control it with copious amounts of alcohol, but it consumed me and took over my life. The worse I felt, the more I pushed everyone away, including my then-fiancée, who tried to help me, but ended up taking the brunt of my frustrations.

Jamie put up with a lot and while I would never physically abuse her, or any other woman, I was an angry drunk and miserable to be around. As the months passed, the attacks continued, and things got incredibly difficult for me. I thought I was losing my mind.

I tried everything I could think of to get better, but nothing was working. There were no books in the base library that could help me, no internet to search my symptoms, and like I said before, none of us had any clue what a panic attack was back then.

I felt lost. I was torn between my strong desire to continue doing my job, and my growing inability to do it right. Things came to a head when I accepted that I wasn't going to get better on my own and I considered the possibility that I could make a fatal mistake. There was nothing left for me to do but report to the Intel Officer and disclose my condition, then voluntarily surrender my security clearance before it was taken from me.

I'll never forget the feeling of that green badge between my fingers after I unclipped it, and how hard it was to let go. In that moment, I knew it was all gone. Everything I had worked so hard to achieve, all my dreams for the future, my reputation.... gone.

I wish I could remember that officer's name, because I owe a great deal to her. She sent me to flight medicine for a checkup and then to see a psychiatrist, though she was very clear about what I could and could not discuss. Ultimately, she protected me from any kind of retribution for leaving the program and ensured that I received the honorable discharge that my service jacket warranted.

My world felt upside down and by that point, all I wanted was to come home. Everything I had worked for was gone and I had no idea why. The psychiatrist gave me no answers about what had happened to me, though in fairness, he only got half the story.

I came home defeated and disgraced because I couldn't tell anybody what I had done or been a part of overseas. Those closest to me knew that I had gone through some sort of breakdown and been sent home. I refused to talk about it with anyone else, which only led to speculation and rumors I tried to ignore.

People mocked me, joked that I "washed out" of the Navy, and I lost most of my friends. Even family members treated me differently, as if they were either afraid of me or embarrassed to be associated with me. I just put my head down and took it because I felt weak and ashamed of the person I had become. I had done everything I was supposed to do and it just wasn't good enough.

My attacks never really went away, but they were much less intense than overseas, and I did my damndest to drink them into oblivion. The nightmares came about a month after I got home, which led to insomnia because I was afraid to go to sleep. That was my new existence.

I coped as best I could with alcohol and even started college at Lock Haven University, trying to stay as active as I could to keep myself distracted. I began having intense daydreams that were like mini movies of things that had happened to me and I would feel the same emotions and physical sensations that I did when they actually happened. One night, I was asleep in my dorm room when the dam broke.

I was in the middle of a terrible nightmare and woke up into a panic attack that was worse than any I'd ever experienced. I was beyond terrified and ran down six flights of steps to escape the building. There was a snowstorm underway outside and those giant snowflakes felt like they were suffocating me. I ended up standing in a near-blinding snow, wearing nothing but a pair of boxer shorts, on the emergency phone with my somebody at my fraternity house.

Other than that, I don't remember what else happened that night. I think somebody took me to the hospital, but I have no memory of it. I woke up the next morning in the room of one of my fraternity brothers, who took me to the campus medical clinic. They called school officials, who put me medical leave and arranged for me to go home and see my family doctor. It was then, three years after I had come home from overseas, that I finally got some answers.

I was diagnosed with panic disorder and depression, then prescribed medicine to help. My doctor explained that the human brain is like pressure cooker and can only hold so much, before it either finds a way to vent and release the pressure, or it explodes. He told me that I had been pushing it down and hoping it would go away for the past three years, but all I was doing was building up more and more pressure. He explained the mechanics of a panic attack, assuring me that I wasn't going crazy.

These days, it seems like the term "panic attack" gets thrown around so loosely in movies and on TV, that they've turned it into a punchline. Only someone who's never experienced an attack would treat it like a minor inconvenience, instead of the hellish torment it truly is.

Billie, I'm not sure if you or someone close to you has ever experienced an attack, so let me share with you how they manifest in my life. It always starts with a vague feeling that something is wrong. I can't quite put my finger on it, but something feels off. That is soon followed by the sensation that I'm walking on springy foam, sinking into the ground with each step. If I'm sitting or lying down, I feel like my head is floating and have no control over the situation.

That loss of control is an underlying theme in every panic attack. There's a brief moment in the beginning when I know what's about to happen, but it suddenly dissipates within seconds, as my world goes dark and I feel trapped inside my own body. My heart seems to be beating as fast as a drummer's sticks during a drumroll and I experience a strong sensation that I can't breathe, which makes me feel like I'm suffocating. No matter how hard I try to take in more air, it's not enough.

By that point, we're firmly underway and I begin to have no idea what's happening to me. I lose access to my long-term memory during attacks and nothing makes any sense. Terror and dread take over my mind as my body runs through the instinctual fight or flight process. I feel an intense need to get out and to escape, no matter where I am.

After about 10 to 15 minutes, as suddenly as it comes on, the attack subsides and I can recognize what I just experienced. There's a wave of relief that washes over me when I realize it's over, which is quickly followed by a monsoon of fear as I remember what's coming next. You see, my attacks aren't just one and done; They almost always cycle over and over, sometimes two or three cycles and sometimes they go on until I pass out from exhaustion.

Typically, when I wake up, I don't remember what happened. I sometimes find notes in my email that I sent to myself from in between cycles.

That's what panic attacks do to me and they come unexpectedly, anytime and anywhere. I equate them to a terrifying demon that follows me around, hiding in the shadows and watching my every move, ready to strike when I least expect it.

The medicines that first doctor gave me made my mind foggy, as did the other varieties we've tried over the years. My current medicine regiment includes one prescription that I swear does absolutely nothing to help me, but the doctors insist I take it, or one of its "sister drugs" in the same class. I've tried several of them and experience has shown me this one has the least side effects, so even though it feels futile, I take it.

My family practitioner, who prescribed the first set of meds, told me not to drink on them, but his advice fell on deaf ears. A few days later, I was sitting around the bar at our local American Legion and I opened up to some Vietnam vets about what I was experiencing. I expected them to give me a hard time or mock me, especially with all that they had been through, but they were supportive and kind to me. One of them gave me contact information for our local VA clinic.

At their urging, I called from the bar and made an appointment. The first VA doctor I saw was a general practitioner, who noted some physical issues that occurred during my military service and then referred me to a VA

Psychiatrist. The Psychiatrist confirmed what my family doctor had told me about Panic Disorder and Depression, and also diagnosed me with PTSD. At the time, I refused to accept the PTSD diagnosis, because I hadn't been in combat and I didn't feel like I had earned it, if that makes any sense.

The VA put me in their system for medical coverage, but I didn't file for any kind of disability until 2000 or 2001. I didn't think the military was to blame for me breaking down and not being able to handle a job that I volunteered to do.

Thankfully, I was assigned a tremendous VA doctor who took the time to talk with me about my feelings. He insisted I file to have my conditions service-connected and told me, "Whether you were a cook or you drove a tank, it doesn't matter. You did not come home the same way you left and that's not your fault. The VA is here to help people like you."

I did file and I was initially rated 50% disabled for both my mental conditions and some physical injuries I suffered in uniform. Most importantly for me, I began seeing doctors who specialized in veteran treatment and interacting with other vets from all different generations. Whenever I gave the condensed and cleansed version of my story to these hardened vets, I always expected to be judged or insulted, but neither has ever happened.

It's been my experience that the only people who ever judged me based on my military service, never wore a uniform themselves. I still felt guilty and while I'm laying it all out there, I might as well tell you that I continue to feel guilty today, because there are veterans who have done so much more than me and suffered in ways I can only imagine. Then, there's all those who made the ultimate sacrifice and never made it home.

That guilt has haunted me every day since 2008, when my disabilities worsened to the point I was no longer able to work and the VA increased my disability rating to 100%. I'm lucky to have a persistent psychologist who constantly reminds me the VA didn't just give me that rating, that my medical and service records justified it and so did the findings of all those different doctors the VA had me see over the years.

Prior to them increasing me to the 100% level, I had to see four psychiatrists/psychologists, along with a medical doctor. It was explained to me that the threshold was especially high because of my age, 33-years-old at the time. The whole thing was a lose/lose situation because they didn't want to have to pay me for the rest of my life and all I wanted, was to be able to go back to work like a normal person.

Billie, it just occurred to me that you might be wondering what happened between 2001 and 2008, that led to my disabilities worsening the way they did. Basically, my alcoholism caught up with me and it got to the point where I went through a fifth of rum or bourbon every day. I had also been eating like a horse and I more than doubled my weight. The doctors called it "self-medicating."

Sitting alone in my bedroom one night, drunken and surrounded by the shattered remains of a dream that had meant so much to me, it all became too much for me to bear. In the early morning of October 26th, 2003, I pulled my 9mm out of its case and loaded it with hollow point rounds. I don't know why I filled the 15-round magazine, since I only expected to fire it once.

Then, I slid the magazine into my pistol and pulled the slide back, chambering a round. I stared at the gun for a few seconds before I picked it up and put it in my mouth. I'll never forget the way the cold steel felt on my lips or the sound the metal made when it scraped against my bottom teeth. I held it there and thought of everybody I had hurt or let down in my life. I put my finger on the trigger, asked God for forgiveness, and then I just sat there with memories overloading my mind. I must have passed out, because I woke up on the floor a few hours later and found the gun on my desk, where I had been sitting.

I realized that I didn't want to die, I wanted to feel normal again and for the pain to stop. I also knew that the next time I got drunk, I would go right back to that terrible place of self-loathing and hopelessness, and I probably wouldn't make it out. With the help of Dad, I quit drinking that day. I've been sober for 15 years now.

Without alcohol to use as a crutch anymore, I was forced to face the demons I had been running from for all those years. I wish I could tell you I slayed the inner dragons like some character on TV, but that's not the ways things work in the real world. My attacks grew worse, I developed agoraphobia and generalized anxiety disorder, and my depression grew more severe. I tried different medicines and more doctors, but nothing worked.

Somewhere around 2009, I finally gave up the fight against the PTSD diagnosis and accepted it as legitimate. The two biggest obstacles for me were the fact that I was not a combat veteran and the wildly unrealistic depictions of it in the media. It took a VA psychologist sitting me down and telling me exactly what PTSD really is.

He went down the list of symptoms that I had, each of which were hallmarks of the disorder. We talked about my nightmares, insomnia, how I get startled and upset very easily, and the way I try to push people away and hide from the world, each of which are classic signs of PTSD.

I never told him about my daydreams because they seemed benign and not relevant. I thought they were related to my anxiety issues, until I shared them with my current psychologist, Dr. Y, during one of my sessions. He was the one who explained to me that they weren't daydreams, they were flashbacks.

There was some protest on my part because I'd seen the movies, where veterans would suddenly snap and find themselves back in the middle of a warzone, hallucinating the experience and believing the people around them were enemy soldiers. Dr. Y looked at me as if he was waiting for me to crack a smile or laugh. He thought I was joking.

I wasn't. I genuinely believed what I had seen in the movies and never considered a flashback could be anything else. At that point, he took the time to go into detail about PTSD and how it manifests in different patients. Dr. Y told me that during his time working for the VA, he treated hundreds of veterans with the same symptoms I had, some who were battle-hardened and others who worked clerical and mechanical jobs.

I began seeing Dr. Y regularly in 2011 and have done so ever since. It's because of him, along with my other doctors and some strong medications, that I am able to have the life that I do today. He's opened my eyes to the fact that people experience trauma in all walks of life and what may seem insignificant or minor to one person, might completely cripple another.

Dr. Y tells me, "It's not a contest to see who suffers the most." Different people handle things in their own way and it's not a matter of being strong or weak, it's just life. All we can do is what's within our capabilities and then trust God with the rest.

As limited as it is, this life is mine and I will continue to be grateful for all the good in it and try to ignore the bad. Nights have always been difficult and I don't imagine that will ever change, but if my days can be at least somewhat productive or filled with the laughter of my wife and children, then I'll count myself lucky.

## Chapter 8

I made my way back up to the room and it took a few hours, but I finally did fall asleep and had a restful night's slumber. The peacefulness and quietude of nature surrounding Trakehner Inn is a welcome break from the noise I've encountered virtually everywhere else. I woke up as Andrea was leaving the room for an early morning hike around the lake.

I swear, that woman is part gazelle. By the time I stood up from the bed and plodded over to the window, she had already walked down the stairs and through the house to the back door, crossed the veranda, and was trucking along the path towards the lake. It made me tired just to think of her energy.

Back up in our room, I grabbed my cane and headed to the bathroom for a quick shower. I don't think I've ever been in such a spectacular bath and it blows my mind to think that ours is one of the smaller rooms. The bathroom has to be at least 10 feet tall, maybe higher, and I love the way you've painted the ceiling a dark blue, making the walls appear to extend into nothingness.

Those radiant blue tiles on the wall are stunning and I've noticed them in other spots around the inn. I can't tell if they're original to the 1890s building or if they were added afterwards. Regardless, they go well with the original giant soaking tub and pedestal sink. It's neat to think of all the people that tub has held in the past 120+ years, from historical figures to celebrities, and regular people like me.

I wondered if any of them pray in the shower like I do. It's a habit of mine that goes back to my college days and I don't know how it started, but it seems appropriate. In the shower, we are completely exposed and vulnerable before God. Sometimes I just talk to Him about my life, sort of using Him as an ethereal sounding board.

Speaking of showers, yours was a nice surprise, with the hand-held nozzle affixed to a bar that allowed it to be positioned at various heights. I put it all the way up, so I felt like I was bathing under a waterfall and the size of the tub gave me a lot of room.

When we are away from home, I typically have a hard time in the showers because of my size. Being heavy the way I am forces me to work through issues that average people would never even consider. For instance, I can't reach all the parts of my body when I bathe, so I have a long brush to help me clean areas like my back and legs.

Most showers are also either too narrow for me or don't have enough room for me to stretch in the way I must, to reach the areas that are still within my grasp. I'm sure you're wondering why I don't just use the brush and sometimes I have no other choice, but the brutal truth is that if I go a few days without the stretching, my muscles contract and it hurts to stretch them out again.

Using the commode is a soul crushing, painful experience for multiple reasons and the way it's positioned in our master bathroom at home, there's a mirror directly across from me. It's always nice to be able to watch my shame and humiliation in the reflection.

Please allow me to address the elephant in the metaphorical room, no pun intended. I have tried to lose weight for over two decades and failed every single time. I've lost and regained the same 150 lbs three separate times. Back in 2008, I fought harder than I ever believed I could and I shared my experience with the world, yet I still couldn't get the job done.

Sometime when you get a chance, Google "Donate My Weight." It was an international philanthropic movement I created that helped feed millions of hungry men, women, and children all over America and around the world. Donate My Weight began with a conversation between Andrea and me, trying to come up with motivation to help me lose weight.

I had proven that I wouldn't do it for myself, because I don't like myself very much, which I feel like someone as astute as you would have gleaned by this point. Andrea suggested I buy five-pound bags of flour for every five pounds of weight I lose, so I could keep them in the house and have a physical representation of the fat that I had shed. It was a solid plan and I said I could donate all the flour to our local foodbank after I was done, which sparked the creation of the Donate My Weight movement.

For every pound of weight I lost, I pledged to donate one pound of food to our local food bank, asking friends and family to sponsor me with their own donations. I created a rudimentary website for the campaign and shared it with my loved ones, then on a lark, send the link to our local NBC station in Philadelphia. The next morning, I was making myself coffee when the phone rang and it was NBC, wanting to come do a story on me.

The came to our home to interview Andrea and me, took some video of us walking around the neighborhood, then aired the story on the evening news. The feedback I received was tremendous and almost immediately, I had others who wanted to sponsor my weight loss with donations. Things took a surprising twist the next night, after my story was shown on NBC affiliates all over the country.

The website logged tens of thousands of hits from unique visitors and my email was deluged with letters of support and encouragement, along with nasty notes from people I'd never met, mocking and insulting me. I tried to ignore those as best I could and focus on the many new people who were interested in helping. Some wanted to sponsor me with donations to their local food banks and others wanted to join me on my weight loss journey to shed some weight.

The campaign continued to grow from there, like a pebble rolling down a snow-covered hill, picking up a new layer each time it turned over. I appeared on radio and tv talk shows, was approached by all the other major networks for interviews, spoke with journalists from several magazines, and I appeared on the Rachael Ray Show.

In February of 2008, I also sent a letter and detailed plan to the producers of NBC's hit weight loss program, "The Biggest Loser," asking them to promote the campaign on their show and help spread the word about what I was doing, to their audience. I heard back from one producer about a week later, who told me he loved the idea and would reach out to me after they had a meeting with the network. I never heard from him again.

Instead, sometime in September or October of that year, they introduced their own program that was line by line, exactly what I had proposed to them, renaming it the "Pound for Pound Challenge" and positioning it as if it were their own creation. It was another one of those moments where I was backed into a corner and I had no choice, but to take it on the chin.

I could have sued them, which would have led to expensive legal bills I couldn't afford and ultimately, their shutting down the program. I'd have gotten my credit, but it would have hurt food banks around the country, along with the millions who depend on those food banks. I would never want to be the cause of something like that.

So, I tried to focus on continuing with my own campaign, as they moved forward with theirs. I celebrated the 44,000+ pounds of food donations I was able to raise and tried to ignore their weekly updates on the millions of pounds of food they were donating. What hurt the most was that as time passed, I began getting nasty emails from people who didn't realize the sequence of things and accused me of stealing the idea from them.

Ultimately, millions of hungry people were fed and a lot of other people lost the weight they had been trying desperately to lose, but I was not one of them. It would be easy to blame those who commandeered my idea or all the pressure that came along with sharing my weight loss journey the way I did, but the responsibility falls on my shoulders.

I failed once again, only this time, it was in front of the world. Without alcohol as a prop, I turned back to food and regained everything I had lost, and then some. That's when my doctors diagnosed me with binge eating disorder.

Different weight loss surgery options were presented to me, but I declined. The last time I had been put under general anesthesia, back in the Navy, I woke up in the middle of surgery. I remember the whole thing vividly, from the music and the shocked gasps, to the people grabbing my arms and strapping me down, as someone put a mask over my face and knocked me back out.

In early 2013, I decided to restart Donate My Weight and I partnered with professional wrestling legend and WWE Hall of Famer, "Diamond" Dallas Page, who founded a program called DDP Yoga. People recognize Dallas as this larger than life presence on TV, a former Heavyweight Champion of the World. To me, he was a friend and mentor.

Dallas constantly tried to motivate and help me, the same way he was helping other professional wrestling stars and some of the top names in sports and Hollywood. I was just an average guy, yet we talked all the time, appeared on a few radio shows together, and did interviews for different newspapers.

He did his best to support me and keep me motivated, but just like before, I embarrassed myself in front of everyone and I failed. I eventually gained all the weight back again. It was humiliating and by this point, even my strongest supporters had lost faith in me, though my wife and children were still right there by my side.

My life had returned to the obvious stares, finger pointing, and mocking comments people my size get when they go out in public. Since I've gained the weight, I've had random strangers tell me I was disgusting, suggest I was trying to kill myself with food, call me all sorts of nasty names, and I even had a VA doctor try to convince me that I didn't love my wife and kids. He told me in a straightforward voice, "You must not love your family, because if you did, you would never have let yourself get so fat."

When that doctor said what he did to me, it was one of the few times I spoke up in my defense. I told him he was out of line, he was unprofessional, and he didn't know a damn thing about me or my wife and children. He simply repeated, "You must not love your family," as if it were some sort of mantra and he was trying to attain inner peace by tormenting others.

I tried to mount comebacks in the years since, but they continually fell apart. In April of this year, I weighed in at just under 500 lbs and it crushed my spirit. I had no idea I weighed even close to that much. I couldn't believe that I had fallen so far. You have to understand that I'm a guy who spent most of his life in great shape.

When I graduated boot camp, I weighed 165 lbs. Sure, I looked like I was all skin and bones, but after working out and adding muscle in Corry Station, I rose to a solid 190 lbs. I have a naturally large frame and broad shoulders, so it suited me well. At 190 lbs, I wore a 32-inch waist with a 43-inch chest.

To look at that scale and realize what I had done to myself, what I had done to my wife and my children, was devastating. Even if I could manage to find a way to accomplish what I've never been able to do before and lose all the weight, I couldn't help but wonder if I'd have a heart attack and die before I ever reached the finish line.

Most people struggle to lose 20 or 30 pounds, a far cry from the 300 pounds I have to lose. Then, even if I somehow managed to pull off that miracle and lose all the weight without killing myself in the process, the odds are stacked against me.

Did you know 97% of people who lose weight through dieting and exercise will gain it all back within three years? That percentage is based on decades of research and the case studies from hundreds of thousands of people.

I have fought so many battles over the years, Billie. I fight every day, just to get out of bed and wade through my molasses life, with as big a smile as I can muster on my face. I have nothing left inside, no strength to take on this battle, no motivation to even make the attempt at defying the odds.

That was the thought reverberating through my head while Andrea was out hiking two and a half miles around the lake and I was struggling to catch my breath after walking down one flight of steps for breakfast.

The same three words kept echoing over and over in my brain, "I am broken."

## Chapter 9

The weather was clear and sunny, so Andrea and I sat on the famous Trakehner Inn veranda for breakfast. We enjoyed the fresh fruit, omelets, and coffee cake you served us, chatting for about an hour and taking in the gorgeous mountain scenery. I could see hints of the lake through the tree leaves and the waterfall was directly in my line of sight.

Since I'm being brutally honest about my life, I might as well tell you I heard about every other word in that conversation and had no idea what we were talking about. Aside from my futile attempts to silence the whole "I am broken" cadence going on in my head, I don't hear very well. I have a condition called Meniere's Disease that has rendered me nearly deaf in my right ear. Andrea is used to it by now, much as I hate that she'd have to become used to something like that, but there's nothing I can do.

Meniere's is an incurable disease of the inner ear that has caused me near-constant unsteadiness and random bouts of vertigo that come on without warning, lasting for anywhere between a few hours and an entire day, then cease as suddenly as they began. That's why I sport the sweet quad cane I saw you eyeing up. I know it looks sharp, with shiny chrome visible from the scratches and areas where my dark blue spray paint has worn off, but don't get any ideas. I need that thing to move around.

My first cane was an all-black, standard one-legged deal. It was nothing fancy, but it helped with joint pain and I have three ruptured discs in my lumbar region, with stenosis and scoliosis. The orthopedic doctor I visited explained to me that I had early-onset degenerative disc disease.

The issues weren't caused by my weight, but it certainly hasn't helped anything. I'd also broken both my ankles in the Navy and never had them properly treated, due to my schedule. Everything is healed up, but they ache here and there, especially when I walk for more than short distances.

My doctors told me the weight was a big part of my pain, leading me to believe that when I lost the weight, my pain would go away. As it turned out, that's not the way it all works at all. It's been my experience that the more weight I lose, the more my back and joints hurt.

On top of everything else physically and mentally wrong with me, about two years ago, blood tests showed I also have rheumatoid arthritis. Contrary to the similar sounding names of osteoarthritis and rheumatoid arthritis (RA), they are very different. RA is actually an autoimmune disorder that attacks the soft tissues around joints and virtually everything else in a person's body, from organs and blood vessels to skin and eyes.

My rheumatologist said they don't know what causes it and believe it may be partly genetic. Regardless of the cause, I tested positive for an antibody the National Institutes of Health uses to "identify patients who are likely to have severe disease and irreversible damage."

That description doesn't exactly inspire confidence for a positive future, but I try not to think of it as I deal with the challenges of today. For instance, I can't drive anymore. My doctors haven't officially taken my license yet, so I could legally get behind the wheel should there be an emergency, though I doubt I ever will.

The Meniere's causes me to get dizzy whenever I quickly turn my head to either side, which leads me to miscalculate turns and roam all over the road. Then, there's my mental conditions, which have put me in some dangerous positions over the year. I grew up in the small town where I live today, have driven the roads thousands of times, yet I managed to get lost in the center of town on the main road. I was about a mile and a half from my house and had to pull over because I had no idea where I was at the time.

It happened again when I was trying to drive to the grocery store from our house, on a road that was my childhood school bus route. I got confused and didn't know where I was. That was an especially terrifying experience, because while I had no clue where I was, I was very much aware that I should know. I remembered riding on my bus thirty years prior but couldn't remember where my house was in the present time.

The last draw came when I tried to drive through our neighborhood on my own. I was bound and determined to prove I could still drive and angry at the thought of losing any more of my life to my conditions. I had my cell phone turned to the map application in case I needed directions and I mentally prepared myself to try and stay calm no matter what happened.

I got less than a quarter of a mile from our house and forgot I was driving. Before you say it, I don't understand either. From what I remember, I wanted to change the radio station and I looked down. I was going through the channels on XM radio and the next thing I knew, I was in my neighbor's front yard. Thank God no people, pets, or other cars were on the road, because it would have been awful.

As my Meniere's progressed, I started falling more. I usually landed on the carpet or could soften the fall by catching myself on a wall or piece of furniture, which usually bruised my ego more than my body. Then, one day while I was trying to gather up some toys in my backyard, I tripped and fell off our concrete patio. The dizziness came out of nowhere and I felt like a top, being twisted by an invisible hand. I ended up landing on my head in the yard and knocked myself unconscious.

I was only out for a few seconds, but I could barely move afterwards and laid there in the grass, contemplating my options. Andrea and the kids were in Virginia visiting her brother and his family. I'm not sure if you remember, but when we sat and talked at the inn, I told you how I typically don't travel very well. I rarely leave the house, except for short visits to places close to us or my various doctor appointments.

As a quick aside, you have no idea how happy I was to learn that Trakehner Inn was less than an hour and a half from our house. You're actually closer to me than the VA Hospital in Wilkes Barre. Had things have gone bad for me with my attacks or PTSD, we could have packed up and quickly gotten home. It's happened a couple times before and we've lost a lot of money on non-refundable trips because of it.

Getting back to the fun knocking-myself-unconscious story, I realized nobody would be around to help me until the next day and my daily medicines were upstairs. I tried to stand up, but my back and neck were killing me, and the vertigo was intense, so I crawled into the house. I grabbed the leftover Chinese in the bag and crawled up the stairs to my bedroom. Everything hurt and let me tell you, there was more than a little profanity flying around the house that night.

Andrea came home the next day as planned, we made a doctor's appointment, and the subsequent MRI showed three ruptured discs in my neck, and damage to one side of my cervical spine with stenosis.

That's the point the VA switched me to an old man quad model. My doctor put in the order and they called me on the phone to go over the options. The man who filled the order assured me it would be a smaller block on the bottom with the four legs, so it was more discreet and not as obvious as traditional quad canes. He also said it would be black like the cane I had already been using.

When I went to pick my new cane up at our local VA Clinic, I couldn't believe what I saw. Aside from the thing being enormous and having a gigantic base, it was shiny chrome that looked like the bumper of a 1950s Chevy Bel Air. That cane sparkled in the sunlight and my family, who was waiting in the car, burst out laughing when they saw it.

I can't really blame them, because I would have done the same in their position. For the entire trip over to the clinic, I had gone on and on about how great this new cane would be and how it would barely be noticeable. I told them it would help me get out more often and move around without having to worry about falling or being the center of attention.

That's what the guy from the VA told me over the phone and he sounded so convincing. I'm not sure if he was just saying that to get me to agree to the quad or if he genuinely planned on ordering the cane he described, then saw my weight and was restricted in what he could do. Either way, all my blather about it on the car ride over gave them plenty of justification for their laughs. The very first thing I did when we got home was paint the shiny monstrosity a respectable Navy blue.

Billie, I'm man enough to admit that my doctors were right and the four-legged cane does provide much more stability. As hard as I fought against it in the beginning, I don't go anywhere without it now. The thing is heavy as lead, which is probably because I'm enormous, and it's become a conversation piece with people who don't know enough not to ask a guy about his cane. I named the cane "Jim" to add some levity and take a little sting out of the whole thing.

Ask my kids about Jim the next time you see them and with giant grins, they'll tell you all about my cane and the places we've gone. I'm on my third set of cane tips and he's all scratched and beat to heck, but Jim is standing tall next to my desk as I write you this letter. He's probably reminiscing about our trip to Trakehner Inn too, in his little metal cane brain.

After breakfast that morning, Andrea, and I took Jim for a walk down to the lake. I knew I wasn't going to be able to hike around it like she did and I'd be lucky to get down there and back, but there was no way I wasn't going to at least try and get as close to the lake as possible.

I led the way, with Andrea by my side, and we promptly ended up at the pool, because I got confused and took the wrong path. I'm pretty sure she knew where we were heading and just let me come to the realization myself. I'm an obstinate guy and it was probably easier than arguing with me about which way we should go.

That's who I am and I'm not proud of it, but I can't figure out how to change. I let the limitations in my life get to me and I am far too emotional for my own good. Have you ever read that book about sweating the small stuff? I do the opposite of what that book teaches people. I sweat the small stuff, the large stuff, and stuff I found on the street that doesn't even belong to me.

Please understand that my wife doesn't automatically back down in every disagreement. I don't want to give you the wrong picture of our marriage. She can give it just as well as she can take it and that's one of the things I love so much about her. Besides, sometimes she doesn't need to tell me I'm wrong, because it becomes exceedingly obvious. Your pool told me I was wrong that morning.

A quick turn and nod of my head was all Andrea needed, to know that I was well aware who would be leading from that point forward. She stepped over the wooden edge of the pool step and we walked through the grass, over the stone pathway.

The walk down to the lake wasn't that bad and I made it there much easier than I expected. What a treat it was, too! As I stood on that pedestrian bridge and listened to the water thunder over the falls, I felt peace in my soul. It was a similar feeling to when I first walked through the front door of Trakehner Inn the day before.

I can't quite explain it and I've tried many times since we've been home, but there is some intangible quality that the lake and your home share. You might think I'm crazy, but I felt it deep down in my heart. I was meant to come to Trakehner Inn and beyond that, I knew I was meant to be standing before those falls.

When I told Andrea how I was feeling, she suggested an alternate way of hiking around the lake that I thought was marvelous. She would slowly drive the route in our minivan and I would ride with my head out the window, taking as many pictures as I possibly could.

We headed back up the path to the inn, which turned out to be quite a bit more difficult than I expected, due to the incline. Andrea and I eventually reached the top and got in the car for our "hike." It may not have been the most conventional trek in the world, but it was thoroughly satisfying and I loved every moment of it.

There were no other cars for almost the entire ride, allowing us the time to linger at every bridge, stream, and opening in the trees that provided panoramic views of that stunning lake. Up until this trip, I had been exclusively a fan of the ocean and there was no place I'd have rather been than at the foot of the Atlantic, inhaling salty air and listening to the waves roar.

Andrea likes the beach, but her favorite place has always been in the woods, by a lake. Some of her fondest childhood memories come from Camp Mosey Wood, a Girl Scout camp in the Poconos that she visited each year. Andrea's love of your local area was what prompted me to plan this birthday trip in the first place.

I wanted to give my wife an opportunity to relive those special memories and take her back to the area where they were created. I also wanted to see the lake and mountains through her eyes, to try and understand the allure this kind of environment had for her.

Riding in the car was depressing, despite how entranced I was in the scenery, especially as we passed bicycle after bicycle and saw all the people hiking the area. There was a sort of battle in my noggin, between the joy and serenity I was feeling in those surroundings, and the perennial negativity that I've allowed to take residence in my brain.

The conflict continued as we drove back up to the inn and sitting in the parking lot, it all came to a head. Andrea had gotten out of the van, but I continued to sit there, thinking. She walked over to me and in the time it took her to get there, the storm clouds in my brain made way for the sun. For the first time in a very long time, everything became clear.

There are many people in this world who have a much more difficult life than me and many others who are living the dreams I once held. I knew I didn't want to be bitter anymore and I didn't want to be jealous of other people. What I really wanted was to be the kind of person who prays for those that are suffering and feels sincerely happy for those who are living well. I wanted to be a better person.

Chapter 10

It was too beautiful a day to stay inside, so after we got back from driving around the lake, Andrea and I decided to explore the vast grounds surrounding Trakehner Inn. Seeing the rolling lawns, the fountain, pavilion and everything else from afar was one thing, but it all takes on a much different appearance from up close. This would turn out to be one of my favorite parts of our visit.

We walked from the parking lot to the area just past the inn's front door, finding ourselves in a much wider grassy lawn than I expected, surrounded by flowering bushes and tall pine trees. I'd read all about the inn and knew the property was nearly eight acres but didn't appreciate how big that actually was. I also learned almost immediately, that there was much more to the Trakehner property than what I found online.

There are times in life when words fall short and rather than looking to them for the answers, we must consider what is written as a guide, searching for ourselves to find the truths that can only be experienced. If I were to tell somebody of our walk around the north lawn, stopping to visit the Tudor-styled gazebo that matches the exterior of the inn, how much would they be missing?

I could go on about the colorful bushes reminding me of the flowers my uncle used to grow in the greenhouses on his farm, the way the aged wood of the pavilion had an Earthy smell that reminded me of Grandpa's pigeon coops, or how the mossy ground in the area looked like an old green carpet I played Legos on in my childhood basement.

Nobody else could ever understand the inexplicable feeling those combined memories evoked inside of me.

Grandpa raced pigeons and he loved his birds. During the week from 9am-5pm, he was President of the Merchant's National Bank in Bangor. In the evenings and on weekends, he was the quintessential family man, sharing his affinity for racing championship pigeons with all those he loved so much.

One of Dad's favorite stories was of asking Grandpa for my mom's hand in marriage. He began the conversation by questioning if there was a pigeon race on June 30th, 1962. When Grandpa answered there was not and inquired about the question, Dad replied that he would like to marry Mom on that day.

The scent in that pavilion and the sights around it were subtle, but enough to awaken those special memories and give me a sensation that only I could ever feel. That's the way I look at our relationships with God and how each one of us experiences his presence in our lives.

To most people, church is where they find God, worshiping in unity with fellow congregants. Some eagerly anticipate weekly services, while others consider them a chore, going because they feel as if they must, like God is taking attendance each Sunday.

My personal belief is that God knows what's in each of our hearts and he is available to us at any time and in any place. A person can go their entire life without ever stepping foot in a church and still have a strong relationship with the Lord. That may be all they need, while others crave the feeling of communion that comes from worshiping together and the strong congregational bonds that are created in the process.

I'm sure you know churches serve the Lord in many ways beyond traditional worship services. There are bible studies, support groups, children's programs, retreats, community outreach, and a whole lot more. My congregation has something called the Von Bora Society, which helps families in times of grief.

The morning after Dad passed away, our Pastor came to the house to comfort us, share his memories, and offer spiritual support. As he left, the Pastor let us know that he would be available anytime we needed him and if we wanted, there were others in our church who were also willing to help.

One night, we received visits from multiple members of the Von Bora Society, each of whom delivered a different course for our dinner that evening. Their meal didn't take away the pain of Dad's sudden loss, but it served as a reminder that we didn't have to bear the pain alone.

I was baptized, attended Sunday school, catechism classes, and I was confirmed at St. John's Evangelical Lutheran Church, in my hometown of Nazareth. That's right, I was raised in Nazareth and believe it or not, I was also born in Bethlehem... on a Sunday. Of course, it's Nazareth and Bethlehem Pennsylvania, but don't take away my fun.

It still counts and as much as I joke about the similarity, I also find comfort with it. My relationship with God is less formal than what tradition may say is appropriate, but I look at the Lord as both a father and a trusted friend.

I talk to God all the time, especially when I'm in nature. That's when I feel the closest to Him, surrounded by the sheer majesty of his creation. As much as I love my church and I do feel close to Jesus within those hallowed walls, there's an entirely different feeling out in nature, particularly when I'm near a large body of water.

I don't know what it is about water, but my most powerful and profound prayer sessions have occurred either directly at the water's edge or with it nearby. This is one of those times when words fall short and I'm unable to explain exactly what I experience. I can tell you it feels as if I'm talking directly to Jesus, who is quietly listening, giving comfort, and gently guiding me in the right direction.

After some contemplation and exploring of the lawn, we headed over to the stables and the north paddock, where you used to train and exercise your horses. I don't know much about horses and the care that goes into them, but Andrea does and she took great pleasure in explaining it all to me.

When she was young, she took riding lessons and grew to love those majestic animals. She had always hoped to have horses of her own one day, but as life became more complicated, that dream got shoved aside. It was such a treat to see the excitement in her eyes as she walked through the horse enclosures in the stable and led me around the paddock area, sharing her stories.

We talked about what it must have been like for you to have your horses boarded right next to your house and be able to ride them anytime you wanted. I imagine it also involved a ton of work, though judging by the way Andrea described it, that care sounded more like a labor of love.

I surveyed at the paddock area and saw the way trees and bushes had sprouted up, reclaiming the territory, but I got the distinct impression that Andrea was looking beyond that and seeing something I couldn't. She talked of stallions trotting around the perimeter and there being obstacles to jump in different areas, which was all hard for me to visualize.

What I did notice was the tender way she spoke about those horses, both the ones she had known and the mental image she'd created of yours, based on what you described to us. It led me to wonder if Andrea also felt God in nature, particularly when she was atop one of those steeds, galloping along, with the wind in her face.

Andrea attends church often and is especially active outside of the summer months, when our children sing in the choir and St. John's holds evening services dedicated to families. I try to come see the kids sing when I am able, but rarely attend services anymore. It's not because I don't want to be there, it's due to the trouble I have being among large crowds.

Our congregation is like another family to me. The daughter of one of my Sunday School teachers is now Director of Youth and Family ministries. Meanwhile, the grandson of another beloved Sunday school teachers is leading a committee to find our church a new Head Pastor, following the retirement of our longtime spiritual leader.

One of my favorite things to do is walk in the nave when it's empty and quiet, sitting on the alter steps and looking out towards the pews. I relive so many special moments that occurred in that sacred space, like the baptisms of my children, services when I was an acolyte and Dad sang in the choir, the weddings of my friends, and Dad's funeral.

Like everything else in life, there's always a balance. For all the pain, there's pleasure. For all the joyous tears shed in our most triumphant moments, there's the sting of salty brine on cheeks raw from the seemingly endless cascade that accompanies our deepest sorrows.

I will always be connected to St. John's through my memories and the love I have for our congregational community, but the church where I feel the closest to my Lord is the one he built. As we walked away from the stables and headed around the Inn, I stopped to lean over and smell the flowers, as trite as that might sound. I'm allergic to pollen, but I love the scent.

The red stone path is surrounded by them on flowering bushes of all varieties. It was about this point that I noticed the first of several areas on the property that were not cleared and left in their natural state. This one was on the side of a steep incline, with a small valley below it, just on the other side of the small cottage.

I noticed a fence encircled the property, running parallel with the boundaries at most points, with the exception these natural habitats. In looking over the rustic wooden barrier, which had become weathered by decades of exposure to the elements, I witnessed a concerto that could only be composed by God himself.

There were a variety of animals scurrying around the bushes and grasses that filled the landscape, with a rhythmic hum of insects buzzing all around, augmented by birds chirping in the tall pine trees above. The air was heavy with the scent of raw life, a woodsy, floral aroma that can only be found in places like this.

The sense of smell is probably the most underappreciated among all of our five senses and yet, it's the one that is most closely linked to our memory. One sniff and poof, we're transported to another place in our mind. For someone like me, that's not always a good thing, but on this day and in that place, it was a great blessing.

The scents took me back to a trail I used to hike at Jacobsburg State Park. It began by a large foot bridge, leading up the hillside and along a cliff that overlooked the surging Bushkill Creek down below. The path eventually led down into the valley, where a natural bridge allowed access to the other side and a rocky slope up to the top.

It never ceased to amaze me how different the same area could appear when comparing cliff views to those in the valley. The same trees, plants, creek and the rest were all still there and visible, but the difference was in the perspective.

Thinking about how the Bushkill Creek made me yearn to be by water and as I scanned the Trakehner grounds before me, I took notice of the large fountain. We headed that way, admiring the south paddock as we walked. I was surprised at how pristine it has remained after the years of disuse.

With the fence still in place and the lush, grassy lawn freshly manicured, it gave the impression that more horses could be coming along to exercise there any day. Andrea, ever the smarter and more logical one between us, explained that you probably use the area for outdoor weddings and other events hosted by the inn. Her reasoning made sense, but I preferred the thought of horses reclaiming their domain.

I love your fountain and the way it appears to be emanating from a natural spring, surrounded by rocks and a few flowering plants. I had my back to the inn and was facing the lake, which allowed me to take in both the fountain and the magnificent splendor of God's great works in the background. Light breezes would occasionally blow some of the fountain's mist in my direction and each time it did, the water caused a sensation as if God reached out and touched my face.

Billie, standing by your fountain, I knew that I was finally where God wanted me to be. I had been meant to come to Trakehner Inn with Andrea, to be inspired by your grounds and to wander them, eventually standing in that precise spot. The Lord had a message he'd been trying to share, and the time had come for me to hear it.

Deep within me, I felt a strong compulsion to go back down to the lake. It was unlike anything I'd ever known before. Even though my knees were aching, and my spine felt like it was ready to give out on me at any point, I decided to take the walk. Looking back, there was no rational reason for me to push myself in that way. I was acting purely on faith.

It was slow going, but Andrea and I eventually made it back to the lake and we stood on the pedestrian bridge overlooking the falls. I was searching in vain for a bench when I heard the voice as clearly in my head as if it had been spoken out loud, "I am here."

I contemplated those words for a minute and questioned, "Who is here?"

The response was almost immediate, "I am."

My face must have given away the turmoil I was feeling inside, because Andrea asked me what was wrong. I debated whether to tell her, because I already felt crazy with all my mental conditions and I didn't want to take it to the next level by telling her I was hearing voices. I stood before the tumultuous, yet incredibly soothing waters of those falls, contemplating it all for a few seconds.

She repeated her question, sounding a little more urgent, so I decided once again to trust my instincts and lay it all on the line. I shared with her how I had been feeling ever since we first reached Trakehner Inn, the peace and serenity that had enrobed my being when we walked through the front door. I told her of how I kept revisiting old wounds and painful memories, along with the unexpected revelations I'd had along the way.

Finally, I ended with the voice I was hearing in my head, not really a sound, but more the sensation of thoughts coming to me. When another person speaks to us, we hear their words with our ears, then our mind interprets what we heard. It wasn't like that. There were words in my head, but nothing had been spoken aloud.

I took a pause to breathe and saw her waiting for me to finish. I figured I had come this far, I might as well go all the way. I shared with Andrea that I had been hearing or feeling that voice, not sure which word is best to describe it, for many years. I explained that up at Trakehner Inn, for whatever reason, it was clearer and more prominent.

Once I was gotten it all out, I jokingly said, "The end." It was an attempt to lighten the situation with a little humor and hopefully, let her know that as crazy as she might think I was, she didn't have to worry about me being dangerous.

Now, I'd like to think I know my wife well and in the few moments before she spoke, which felt like it was taking way too long for her to be thinking anything positive, I tried to anticipate what she might say. She's not a cruel person and wouldn't hurt me on purpose, but she also knows I value her honest opinion. I couldn't get a feel for what was coming, but nothing would have prepared me for what she said.

It began with her telling me she felt the same way as I did about Trakehner Inn. The sensation came over her when we drove past the waterfall where we were currently standing and that feeling of tranquility only grew stronger throughout our visit.

"Good start," I thought to myself.

It went a little dark after that, as she mocked me unmercifully for falling in love with the lake. I've written hundreds of magazine articles and a couple books about the beach, providing plenty of fodder for her good-natured teasing. Andrea insisted she had converted me from an "ocean guy" to a "lake guy."

"A bit much," I thought, "But she's not completely wrong," Meanwhile, I was still waiting for her to comment on the voice with increasing impatience. I pondered whether she was going to suggest I tell my psychologist about it, or if she was going to make another joke. I can normally read my wife well, but I was at a loss and trying to keep calm as she slowly began to speak again.

"Have you ever considered the voice you're hearing is God?" Andrea asked. "You talk to him all the time, but do you ever listen when he tries to answer you?"

I began to argue that it couldn't be God, noting my insignificance among the billions of people in our world. She cut me off, quietly singing the opening verse to one of my favorite songs, "Who Am I" by Casting Crowns. That impromptu serenade was all it took for Andrea to make her point and completely challenge the way I looked at myself.

**Who am I, that the Lord of all the Earth**
**Would care to know my name**
**Would care to feel my hurt?**
**-Casting Crowns**

## Chapter 11

One of the highlights of our trip was sitting down and talking with you about your family. I know the inn was booked solid that weekend and you probably had a laundry list of other things you needed to do, yet you took the time to sit with us and share some of your family history.

It's a shame we didn't have more time to talk, because I would have loved hearing more about your parents and what led them to pick Trakehner Inn as their family home. As I sat in the central parlor playing board games with Andrea, I couldn't help but look to my right, into the ballroom, and wonder what it must have looked like when you were growing up.

I envisioned it as a formal living room, with couches on either side of that giant fireplace, conversational seating elsewhere in the room, and the white Steinway baby grand piano in the same corner it inhabits today. Andrea thought it might have been a family room where everyone gathered to talk, watch television, play games, and basically enjoy each other's company.

Either way, we both imagined that room must have been the center of activities during the holiday season. It's not hard to visualize a giant Christmas tree in there, surrounded by presents and maybe even an old-fashioned Lionel train set.

I have two of them, one that I bought years ago and another that was Dad's when he was a boy, dating back to the 1930s. I had them both running a couple Christmases ago and they were a big hit with the kids. Once Angelica began crawling, I decided to keep them in storage for a few years, until she was old enough to know not to play with them.

Family is the most important aspect of our lives, because both Andrea and I were blessed to have been brought up in large, loving families. The further we went down the wormhole of what we thought Trakehner Inn might have looked like when you were younger, the more we talked of how our own family traditions might have looked if we had been raised there too.

Holidays were particularly special in my family, with each of my aunts and uncles hosting a specific one every year, along with my grandparents and parents. We had special family traditions for every holiday and though some of our loved ones are no longer with us and a few traditions have been lost along the way, most still continue to this day.

The first big family holiday we celebrated together each year was Easter, hosted by my Uncle Frank and Aunt Diane. The day would begin with my brother, sister, and I searching our house for baskets and eggs that had been hidden by the Easter Bunny. He was pretty good and even stumped my parents a few times.

I remember one year in particular, he had hidden a hard-boiled egg in the folds of the fancy curtain that hung in our living room. We didn't find it until the summer. It had a bit of an odor by then and what started as a search for "that horrible smell" ended in one of the funniest moments of my childhood. My mom's face was hilarious when she figured out what had happened.

On a normal year, we'd find all the eggs and our Easter baskets, sneak a couple of my mom's homemade peanut butter eggs, then quickly get changed for Sunday School and church.

We always made some neat craft in Sunday School, then church would start, and I'd sit in the pew, doing everything I could not to lose my mind as the excitement built up inside me. It would eventually end, then we'd head home to grab the baked beans Mom perennially took to the family Easter celebration. It was a well-oiled process, except the year Dad accidentally turned on the wrong oven as we were getting ready to leave the house

Our kitchen had two wall ovens and Mom typically only cooked in the top one, except for holidays and special occasions. The bottom oven was used to store our bread and snack foods like potato chips, which is exactly what was in there that faithful Easter morning. Luckily, someone noticed the melting plastic smell and we avoided a disaster. As an added bonus, we were all treated to the sight of burning potato chips through the little oven window.

Once we reached my uncle and aunt's house, the weather played a big part in what happened next. On nice days, my aunt and uncle would have another egg hunt in the backyard for my cousins and me. On rainy days, the adults would sit and talk upstairs, while the kids found something to do in the basement. Honestly, both were win-win for me, because I was just happy to be there.

Dinner time would come and in my earliest memories, my two great-grandmothers would lead the way, followed immediately by my Pappy, who appreciated the allure of a nice smoked ham. There was always plenty of food for dinner, accompanied by all sorts of desserts, then I'd play with my cousins until it was time to go home.

That's when Nana and Grandpa would give all the kids our annual Easter present. It was a giant crushed peanut egg, enrobed in chocolate and emblazoned with our name in white icing. They were handmade at Callie's Candies, a local candy store that's been around for many generations. The store is now called Chocolates on Broadway and just last week, I won a free box of candy in a contest celebrating the "new" owners' 40th anniversary in business.

Nana was the greatest cook that ever lived, as far as I'm concerned, and she made everything from homemade pickles and applesauce to the most amazing cream puffs, eclairs, and other baked goods. Nana's signature entrees would rival a premier restaurant menu and her pot roast was legendary.

Throughout the summer, Nana and Grandpa would always find reasons to host picnics at their house and they'd invite their friends, along with the entire extended family. Uncle Dean would cook burgers and hot dogs on the grill, accompanied by an assortment of Nana's homemade creamed cabbage, potato salad, pasta salad, and more. Dessert would be whatever she felt like making that day and typically included at least two fresh fruit pies and something with chocolate.

If a person didn't know how to play beanbags or quiots when they came, they'd be well acquainted with the games by the time they left. Grandpa would act as master of ceremonies and mingle among the guests, making sure everyone had a fresh drink and partaking in a few himself. The younger folks divided our time between swimming and eating, though my uncle liked to mix things up by running down the hill behind the pool and doing a forward flip into it.

Eventually, the summer would come to an end, leading into the playoff season of holidays. It began on Halloween and although our only real tradition was to eat pizza for dinner and trick or treat, we made our own special memories.

I didn't grow up in a house with a lot of money and on Halloween, we typically dug into a big bag of masks, costumes and wigs that had been amassed over the years. From that grab bag, we'd come up with some sort of fun combination.

Occasionally, my sister and I would think outside the box, like the year I wore her varsity cheerleading outfit and she dressed like a football player. I carried my candy in her megaphone and I think the neighbors appreciated my courage, because I took in a big haul that year.

After Halloween came Dad's favorite holiday, Thanksgiving. Every year, we'd eat the same foods, enjoy the same traditions, and most importantly of all, we would spend quality time as a family. When I was older, Dad explained why that holiday meant so much to him. He told me the cold weather kept everyone together inside, there was no commercialism associated with Thanksgiving, and the day was specifically dedicated to being with our loved ones and appreciating all the blessings in our lives.

Thanksgiving always began with a family breakfast, then the Macy's Thanksgiving Day parade on TV. Afterwards, we'd pack up the baked corn Mom made every year and head off to my Uncle Craig and Aunt Allison's farm. The property had been passed down through my uncle's family and when I was a boy, his parents still owned it.

They lived in a house on one side of the land and my aunt and uncle lived in a colonial era farm house on the other side. It was in that wonderful old home where we all came together each year for our family celebration. We had the traditional Thanksgiving favorites, along with Nana's oyster filling and my aunt's homemade creamed cabbage. I couldn't imagine celebrating Thanksgiving without either one.

All these years later, our family still gathers at the farm to celebrate together, though some of the great ones have gone home to Heaven and we've welcomed newer additions into the mix. Speaking of additions, my aunt and uncle enlarged their house several times, though they always took care to respect the original building. It remains at the heart of their "new" home, with the plaster removed from one wall, exposing the original hand-hewn lumber.

Before I move on from Thanksgiving, I have to mention dessert, which has always been made up of a combination of homemade treats and selections my uncle picked up from a great bakery near the farm. Andrea's family had a tradition of getting together before Thanksgiving and baking pumpkin pies, using a secret family recipe. She brought one of those pumpkin pies to our first Thanksgiving with my family.

The response was overwhelmingly positive, yet I still watched nervously as Nana cut herself a slice. She looked it over, slowly tasted a forkful, then declared it the best pumpkin pie she'd ever had. That was high praise coming from Nana and we've brought one of those pies every Thanksgiving since. Nana may be 95 years old now, but she still looks for Andrea's pumpkin pie.

As we leave my aunt and uncle's house after Thanksgiving, the Christmas season begins for our immediate family. Andrea will not allow us to play Christmas music or place even a single decoration one second sooner. I like to complain, because I know it's a pet peeve of hers and sometimes I enjoy getting her all riled up, but truth be told, I agree with her.

When I was a boy, we had to wait even longer, until December 6th. My sister's birthday was the 5th of December and as much as Mom looked forward to Christmas, she felt my sister deserved her own day of celebration like the rest of us.

Christmas was my mom's favorite holiday and she decorated our house in an elaborate process that took several days. Each room had its own theme for the decorations. Our family room was for Santa decorations and the more whimsical pieces of my mom's collection, like vintage toys and a neat music box that featured a snowy theme and a little magnetic ice skater who skated to the music.

Our kitchen was decorated with Swedish hand-crafted pieces in honor of my unofficial Swedish sister, Anna, who we originally welcomed into our family as an exchange student when I was a little boy. She captured everyone's hearts and by the time Anna had to go home, she had carved her own place in our family tree. I love her like I love my actual sister and she's come back to visit several times. Mom also made the trip to visit Anna in Sweden.

The formal living room and dining room were reserved for religious decorations and our family's nativity creche. The one exception to that rule, was my mom's collection of Duncan Royale Christmas figurines, which she kept in the living room display cabinet, safe from kids and the dogs, who were trained not to go into our living or dining rooms.

Those figurines remained up all year and it was her way of always keeping Christmas in her heart. Half were religious in nature and the others were versions of Santa from around the world. Over the family room hearth hung an embroidered piece in a gilded frame that probably best explained why Mom loved Christmas so much. It declared simply, "Christmas is Love."

Our family celebrated Christmas with two-days of festivities that began at Nana and Grandpa's house, where everyone would gather on Christmas Eve. Their home featured a gorgeous oversized stone fireplace, with a mantel made of reclaimed wood from a historic bridge that had been town down. The same stones that adorned the fireplace were used to build the entire exterior wall that ran the length of the room.

The adults had their cocktails as the kids enjoyed soda and the joyous, festive atmosphere. Two of my grandparents' closest friends, Winnie and Mavis, were the hit of the party every year. They would thoroughly enjoy their holiday spirits, laughing and joking with everyone all night, before heading off to church.

Like every other event Nana catered, the food was amazing. Each Christmas Eve, we got to enjoy two of the greatest culinary delights ever to leave her kitchen, clam pie and homemade chocolate fudge. The clam pie would be served with dinner and as I write this, I can actually close my eyes and taste the rich clam filling and buttery crust. Nana's fudge recipe had been passed down to her and each year, she'd make it from memory.

There was a wooden sled that Nana filled with all different varieties of homemade cookies, which we'd enjoy with big classes of milk and a healthy dose of fudge. After everyone was festively stuffed, we'd gather around the piano to sing Christmas carols. There was one year when we altered the tradition, and, on that night, Nana and Grandpa taught me a lesson I've never forgotten.

I was thirteen years old at the time and members of our extended family were dealing with a terrible loss. In their grief, they had decided to skip the festivities and stay home. My grandparents knew they were hurting and wanted to do something to remind them that they were loved and help bring a little peace to their hearts. Nana wrapped up some cookies and fudge, then we all packed into cars and headed over to their house.

We gathered by their front door and began singing some of the more reverent carols. Everyone was tentative at first, but we quickly rose in unison. That was the only time in my life I ever caroled outside someone's house.

I was standing by the door when it slowly opened. At first, they looked sad and confused, but as we continued to sing, the tears began to flow. Nana and Grandpa hugged them first, then we all followed. Before I knew it, everyone was crying, myself included.

It was powerful moment and in it, I learned the true meaning of Jesus's command to "Love one another as I have loved you." I truly believe on that night, God directed my grandparents to be an instrument of his grace, while also teaching the rest of us through their example.

The mother told us of her prayers for relief from the pain and while there was nothing we could have done to heal that grieving family, God did answer her prayer, and provided the family a show of love to remind them that they didn't have to go through it alone.

It was on that night, Christmas Eve 1988, that I learned the true power of prayer. I also learned that God has different ways of answering prayers and sometimes the angels he sends aren't angels at all. Billie, have you ever considered how many times you've been a savior to someone in need without even realizing it, or an answer to a prayer that you never knew was asked?

Speaking of a savior, I can't go on without sharing my family's Christmas Day traditions. That's always been the greatest day of the year for me and sure, I've gone from a little boy celebrating Christmas to the daddy of a little boy celebrating Christmas, but the magic in the air feels just as real and that Christmas love still flows through my veins each season.

As a child, every year I'd wake up sometime around 4am, try to convince my parents to go see if Santa came, then get sent back to my room to sleep a little longer. The cycle would repeat itself several times until I finally wore them down around 6am and they gave up. Mom would always go downstairs first to check if he came.

It wasn't until I became a parent that I realized that check entailed getting a camera ready and turning on the tree lights. Mom lived for this morning, almost as much as my brother, sister, and me. As we made our way down the stairs and walked into the family room, that flash would go off in rapid succession. She craved that "Wow!" moment.

Mom has always been a gift-giving champion, going out of her way to find the perfect present for everybody on her list. She'd make her choices, keep track of store sales, then run at it like it was her job. Her Christmas shopping began December 26th and continued through the year.

Then, on Christmas morning, she would anxiously watch the faces of whoever was opening their gift, trying to figure out if they liked it. Getting a smile was all she needed to be happy, but when there was an excited utterance or wide-eyed enthusiasm, she was living the dream. It made her happy to make those she loved happy and Mom has always had a natural talent for it.

Even today, she takes great satisfaction in getting the right gift and when one of her grandchildren shouts in joy, that smile on her face is as bright as the lights on the tree. The delight Mom takes in making her family and friends happy is one of my favorite aspects of Christmas and a big part of why the experience is so special to me.

After we opened up presents, we'd have our traditional egg soufflé, together as a family. It's an egg and cheese dish that is prepared the night before and then baked in the morning. I didn't learn until I was older that when she was checking to see if Santa came, she was also preheating the oven. Once the egg soufflé came out, the double-smoked ham went into the oven.

My Sunday school teacher owned a local meat market and every year, she'd get her hams from him. I don't know what all is involved in smoking or how my mom's low and slow cooking method helped, but what I do know is that when those hams came out of the oven after about 6 hours, the kitchen was filled with relatives all anxious to try a bite.

My aunt Allison taught me about the fine delicacy that is smoked ham fat. It tastes like a creamy piece of bacon that melts in your mouth. If that doesn't sound like something you'd enjoy, then I'm not sure we can be friends anymore.

Christmas day was Mom and Dad's turn to shine, because it was the holiday when my entire extended family came to celebrate at our house. The old Miller homestead was filled with laughter, the singing of Christmas carols as Dad played the piano, and an indiscernible sense of contentment mixed with happiness.

Every year, Mom made about 10 different varieties of Christmas cookies, including cut-outs in gingerbread, chocolate, and vanilla, along with my personal favorite, kiss cookies. They're basically Hershey Kisses in the center of a puffy peanut butter cookie and their existence is further proof of the love God has for mankind.

The amount of work involved in making all those cookies was outrageous, but she'd start right after my sister's birthday and store them in tins. Then, when Christmas day came, she would pull out her own sled cookie holder that was identical to Nana's and fill it to the brim. We were allowed to have as many as we wanted, and a day filled with presents and unlimited cookies was a good day to be a kid.

One thing you might have noticed missing from our Christmas Day celebration was a visit to Church. We typically went on Christmas Eve and not Christmas Day. The candlelight services at my church were particularly moving.

That's not to say we didn't worship or pray, just that we didn't do it in church. Before each holiday meal there was always a prayer and throughout all our family gatherings, members of my family would speak openly about their faith.

It was a powerful thing to experience as I was growing up, because my family didn't typically quote scripture or use it in everyday conversation. They could have done it if they wanted but instead, they would talk about God like he was a member of the family, sitting in the room with us. They'd tell stories of things that happened or times in their life when they felt closest to Jesus. Hearing people I loved and respected, talking openly of their love for the Lord, made a strong impression upon me.

Nana was particularly great at starting those conversations. As a Methodist, she would preach and speak the Gospel during services, along with called and ordained ministers. I have a notebook filled with her sermons and as a boy, I'd go with her to record daily Bible messages on her congregation's "Dial A Prayer" answering machine.

Dad's father, my Granddad, went to seminary and although he eventually left the church to pursue a career in business, he remained steadfast in his relationship with God. His brother continued on the path, becoming an ordained minister in the Unitarian faith and later, a Doctor of Divinity.

Distance separated us from Dad's side of the family and we saw them only once or twice a year, but I have a few of my Granddad's sermons as well. They serve as a reminder of the faith that flows like sap through both sides of my family tree. Dad was the one who taught me as a boy, that I could talk to God at any time or in any place, because He was always with me.

## Chapter 12

It was a bittersweet moment as the end of a lovely day drew near. The sky commenced its nightly changing of the guard, with the sun gently surrendering its position as the moon rose to take its place. I'd go into detail about how beautiful of a show they put on for us, but I'm sure it's old hat to you.

I had begun the day immersed in the negative aspects of my life, dwelling on only one side of my past and present. As the day progressed, so too, did the scope of my introspective lens. The details of my life hadn't changed, but my perspective had.

Sitting on the Trakehner Inn veranda, watching the sunset with Andrea, I talked to God again, thanking him for leading me to this special place. He answered me, though not in the way I expected.

Having learned from my experience this morning at the lake, I eagerly waited for that voice to respond and provide me a sense of hope or some sort of direction for the future. It didn't come. I closed my eyes, trying to clear my head and listen as hard as I could, but there was no voice. All I could here were random noises on the lawn in front of me.

When I opened my eyes, I saw something that took my breath away. Two deer, a buck and a doe, had walked out of the woods and were playing on the south lawn, directly in front of us. Judging by their body size and the smaller antlers on the buck, they seemed to be only a few years old. Andrea had already taken notice and was entranced in the display. I joined her, watching these magnificent creatures acting like two lovestruck teenagers.

The doe was standing there, surveying the landscape and the buck seemed to be doing everything he could to get her attention. At one point, he was running in circles around her, periodically stopping to bow in her direction. Like any female playing hard to get, she would occasionally look his way, then turn and go back to her business.

This continued for several minutes, before she started to walk away, parallel to our position. He paused to eat some leaves off the tree, before following her. Then, he abruptly stopped and looked in our direction. The doe stopped walking as well, though she seemed more interested in a squirrel that had run past her.

The buck did the exact opposite of what I expected, and he walked right towards us, stopping about 20 feet from the veranda. He was a bold young buck. At that point, I slowly and carefully turned on my camera and took off the lens cover.

I wanted to immortalize the moment and have images we could look back on in the years to come. Besides, I knew nobody would believe me if I didn't have pictures. I changed a few settings to account for the lower light of dusk and when I looked up, his rear end was facing me. The buck wasn't spooked as I initially thought and instead, he was slowly walking back over to the doe.

I did my best with pictures, but the dusk setting gave everything a blueish hue and when I changed it to the sunset setting, the deer were so dark they blended in with the background. Time was wasting and Andrea told me I was going to miss them, so I turned on the automatic settings and snapped as many shots as I could.

Most were blurry, but I did manage to get a few good ones of the buck eating some more leaves and the doe looking entirely disinterested in everything he was doing. We watched for a little longer, before the two of them turned and slowly walked off into one of the natural areas of the property, side by side.

Andrea and I followed them, keeping our distance, but I got distracted by the fountain and found myself standing next to it, mesmerized by the streams of water. That's when it occurred to me just how many different animals we had seen on the Trakehner Inn property over the course of our short stay.

There were geese milling around the south paddock and then walking down the path earlier that morning, countless small birds and butterflies of many variety had maintained a constant presence, a lone hawk was circling from the lawn to the lake and back, plus we encountered many rabbits, chipmunks, and squirrels.

In one of the funniest moments of our trip, I was in the pool earlier in the day, while Andrea read in a poolside lounge chair. We both heard squeaking sounds and looked over to see a little chipmunk chasing a squirrel across the top of the rock wall that separated the pool area from the veranda. I think they were playing, because that squirrel was twice his size.

The chipmunk later emerged and sat on the rocks, watching Andrea and me. Despite growing up in Pennsylvania and being around all kinds of nature throughout my life, I'd never seen a chipmunk before. I climbed out of the pool and he didn't move, so I went for my camera. When I turned around, he was gone.

I love animals, though I'm not especially fond of snakes and large lizards. Little ones don't bother me and when I was overseas, there were geckos all over the place. They seemed to especially love hanging out on the exterior walls of my house. They didn't bother me, and I left them alone.

The same went for the snakes, which seemed to love suddenly slinking through the grass when I least expected it. I'm not even embarrassed to tell you I would jump more often than not. Luckily, I never encountered any large ones in the wild.

They're fine at zoos and I enjoy seeing them behind glass, where I can appreciate the beauty of their markings without worrying about getting bitten or one tricking my wife into eating an apple. It's not that I'm afraid of snakes. I'm embracing my inner Adam.

I do love animals, both those free in nature and the loyal, loving pets I have known throughout my life. My parents had a special affinity for St. Bernards and for most of my childhood, there was always one padding around our family home, along with a few cats.

They are a gentle breed, despite their size, and saints are among the most affectionate dogs you could ever know. Yes, they slobber, and they love to give big, wet kisses, but it's all part of their charm. There's nothing like a big fluffy dog that you can hug to your heart's desire. They thrive on the attention and the more love you show a saint, the more love they'll give back to you.

Over the course of my childhood and teenage years, our family had four of them. One of the sad realities of St. Bernards is that their lifespan isn't as long as other dogs and their giant size makes them susceptible to certain diseases and other medical conditions.

The first saint we had after I was born was Mandy, a beautiful long-haired girl who loved to sit in the recliner near the fireplace. I'm not sure how it happened, but that became her spot and she could sleep there for hours at a time. Her one quirk is that she loved to run and if we didn't have the leash on securely when we took her outside, she'd take off like a lightning bolt.

I was about five years old when Mandy was diagnosed with cancer and my parents did what they could to help her, but it reached a point where nothing more could be done. That was when Dad explained to me his feelings on euthanasia with pets.

He said, "Benji, they give us their love freely, trust us to take care of them, and when they need us the most, we have a responsibility to do the right thing. No matter how much it hurts to say goodbye, it would be selfish to make them suffer, so we could have them around a little longer." I would go on to embrace that philosophy myself and teach it to my own children.

After Mandy, came Gussy. We got her as a little puppy and raised her in our home. She was a short-haired saint with huge jowls that oozed more slobber than any dog I've ever known. Gussy was a sweetheart with a gentle and kind disposition. We would let her off the leash outside and she'd follow us all over the yard, just happy to be around my family.

Gussie's death was difficult, because she only lived a little over three years. One day, she began having seizures and the vet diagnosed her with epilepsy. It was an especially difficult blow, with someone close to our family also struggling with the same disorder.

The seizures Gussie experienced were known as "grand mal," meaning she would lose complete control of herself, fall down, and violently thrash around. Afterwards, she was disoriented and felt like she had done something wrong, cowering in corners or hiding in other rooms. It was heartbreaking to watch.

Mom and Dad tried to help her, but one day, she had a seizure and flung herself into a glass patio door. By the grace of God, the glass didn't break and she wasn't seriously injured. It could have easily gone the other way and my parents knew that one day, it almost definitely would. Between the glass doors, staircase, and a host of other hazards, we all feared for Gussie and anyone who was around her when the seizure happened.

It was clear what my parents had to do, but that didn't make it any easier or less painful. Dad took her to the vet's office alone, just as he had done with all our family pets in the past. He stayed with her and kept her comfortable in those final moments.

After we lost Gussie, it would be years before we welcomed another saint into our house. His name was Austin and he made his own impact in our lives. Years later, he was followed by our family's final saint, Annie. Mom and Dad never intended to get another dog, but one day, our local newspaper did a feature on a family with a female St. Bernard who had given birth to 14 puppies in one litter.

They included a picture of the mother feeding the 14 puppies, with the headline, "Bernice and her Brood." Mom saw that picture and it captured her heart. She showed it to Dad and they both agreed the scene was incredibly cute, but their days of raising puppies were over. That's when I entered the picture...

I talked on and on about those puppies, trying to convince my parents to adopt one. It was to the point that I drove Mom and Dad so crazy, I'm pretty sure they only agreed to go see the puppies, solely to shut me up. On the other hand, as stubborn as Mom could be when she'd made up her mind about something, I knew she always had a soft spot for saints.

It's difficult to say what motivated them to go see those puppies, but while they were there, they ended up putting a deposit down on one. A few weeks later, Annie was old enough to come home. With all their kids relatively grown up, Mom and Dad spoiled that dog beyond belief. She soaked up all the love she could get and turned out to be the sweetest and most loving of all our saints.

When old age caught up with Annie and she had reached the end of her life, we tried different things to ease her pain. Her condition worsened to the point where she could barely move and pain medicines only served to make her loopy and uncomfortable. The decision was made to take away her pain and help Annie cross over to Heaven. I knew she would be in good hands once she got there, because she had outlived Dad.

In her final moments, it was me lying on the floor next to Annie, holding her head in my arms and rubbing her as the tears cascaded down my face. When she closed her eyes for the final time, I held her tight, kissed nose over and over, telling her to "go see Daddy."

A year later, once the sting of that awful day had faded, Andrea and I decided to get a St. Bernard of our own, to welcome into our new family. We already had two cats that Andrea adopted just prior to meeting me, both rescues that had been found abandoned on the street.

Andrea and I felt strongly about doing the same with our dog, adopting a saint that needed a good home, rather than buying one from a breeder or pet shop. We found Sasha in an SPCA just outside of Philadelphia and she was in terrible shape when we got to her. She was infested with fleas and some intestinal bug, had large, infected open wounds on her back, was missing big patches of her fur, and she was uncomfortable around men.

Our vet gave her medicine in the office, cleaned and sanitized her wounds, then sent us home with a regiment of pills and creams. It was a bit of a difficult adjustment period for her and the first time we left her alone, we came back to find she had eaten most of our linoleum kitchen floor.

After that, things calmed down and with training and regular walks, Sasha transformed into the ideal pet for our family. Unfortunately, her rough early years took a toll on her body and after seven and a half years, she began to struggle with the same problems that plagued Annie.

It was the first time I was involved with making that difficult decision, but I remembered what Dad taught me all those years ago. It was about doing what was best for her, not me. When the time came, I got down on the floor with Sasha too, held her head and told her how much I loved her as she drifted away.

After some time passed, we chose to adopt again and took in two three-year-old dogs from the Saint Bernard Rescue Network. One was a short-haired female named Emma, and the other was a long-haired male named Dakota. Both came from different homes with much different backstories, but when they reached us, we made sure that the were given the life they deserved.

The two bonded almost immediately and took on a big brother-little sister mentality. Emma was phenomenal with our children and loved snuggling. She was so good that my youngest daughter, Angelica, learned to pull herself up to a standing position by holding onto Emma. When she began walking, it was Emma who made her feel safe enough to take those first steps.

Meanwhile, Dakota was my buddy and he loved to lay with me. There was something very intuitive about that dog and he could sense when an attack was coming or when I was going through a particularly difficult stretch. He wouldn't leave my side during those times and he became overly affectionate.

We lost both of them last year and it was devastating. Emma developed stomach cancer the year prior, but she fought for seven months. Once she reached a point where she could no longer eat from her bowl and struggled to stand up, we ended her suffering. Like Annie and Sasha before her, she was cradled in my arms when she left this world, getting a belly rub and soaked in tears.

Later in the year, we woke up one day to find that Dakota had thrown up in 12 different locations around the house. He was lethargic and his eyes were glassy, so we rushed him to the animal hospital. It made no sense, because he had been perfectly fine the day before, but when they weighed him, we learned he had lost about 30 lbs. We never noticed, because he had that big fluffy mane of fur.

The doctors gave IV fluids to hydrate him and a broad-spectrum antibiotic that would help virtually any infection he might have. They also took blood and promised to get back to us later that night. Around 9pm they called and said his blood work looked better than they expected, but there was a problem with his pancreas. They believed it was a tumor and said they would need additional tests to know more.

We brought him up to our bedroom and he was laying on his bed in the corner as we watched television. Around 11pm, I went over to lay with him and see if he was doing any better. The blankets were soaking wet, but I thought it was likely drool or at worst, he had peed. Then he suddenly stood up and moved towards our bathroom, as his bowels let loose multiple times.

Andrea grabbed him and led him downstairs to go out, while I flipped on the light to clean up the mess. That's when I saw that it was all blood. There was no fecal matter, just blood everywhere, on the floor, on his bed, and on me. Andrea heard me yell when I realized it was blood and quickly came up to trade places with me. I took my Big Fluff outside, held him and cried, because I knew I was about to lose him too.

The animal hospital was closed, so I called a 24-hour emergency vet in a neighboring town, while Andrea woke up our oldest daughter to watch the other kids. Andrea told me on the way over that there was blood all over the hallway too, and she had just covered everything with towels. We had wall to wall carpeting and there really wasn't much more she could do.

Dakota made it to the hospital and I did my best to explain to the doctor what happened, but she misunderstood at first and thought it was just blood in his stool. When I told her about our earlier appointment and clarified that it was all blood, she realized the situation. They took Dakota into a back room for a checkup, then had us meet him in a quiet area, where Andrea said her goodbyes.

I got down on the ground once more, had to physically lift his head up to put it in my arms, and I held him as he went to be reunited with Emma. He lost a lot more blood in there and I tried to ignore it, rubbing his head and kissing his nose until he was gone. The doctor from the animal hospital called me back later in the week and confirmed he had an aggressive form of metastatic pancreatic cancer. By the time the symptoms are recognizable, it's too late.

I loved each of those dogs like they were my own children and grieve for them daily, but I also know their pain is gone and I will see them again one day. It's a good thing I'm typing this and not writing it out on paper, because I've been sobbing since I talked about Annie's final moments.

My newest furry child is sitting on the floor staring at me, wondering what's wrong. Last December, we adopted three-year-old Zoey through the Saint Bernard Rescue Network. She's wonderful with our actual kids and loves to snuggle with me on the couch.

As hard as it is to say goodbye, I know that we provided a good home to each one of those saints, just as we will do for Zoey. There's intense pain and tremendous love involved in these pet relationships, especially when adopting an older giant breed dog, but I would rather focus on the love. That's what it's all about.

Chapter 13

The sun had risen once again, and it was our last day at the Trakehner Inn. Andrea didn't go for her hike this morning because we began talking and lost track of the time. Before we knew it, several hours had passed and it was time to go downstairs for breakfast.

This trip has come full circle in ways I could never have anticipated. When the plans were made, it was all about Andrea and doing something special for her birthday. I thought she'd be able to reconnect with the mountains, woods, and waterways that had captured her heart as a child.

Andrea's parents loved nature and often took her brother and her camping. They'd also go hiking at places like Glenoka Falls and take frequent walks in the various parks surrounding her home in of Allentown, PA. She knows every inch of those local parks and one of my favorite things to do in the early days of our relationship was to accompany her on walks, listening to her stories.

As cliché as it may sound, we literally stopped to smell the roses on many occasions. The walking path at my favorite park led through the most exquisite rose gardens, vibrant with a multitude of colors that emanated from hundreds of perfectly manicured bushes and climbing varieties. The climbers were ensnared on ornate trellises, with their thorns and buds overtop of us as we walked underneath.

Their awe-inspiring appearance was only overshadowed by the fusion of fragrances that imbued the air with what I imagined to be the of aroma of sanctity. I enjoyed each of our walks, but those that led through the rose garden were the best and when we moved away from Allentown, I planted my own little rose garden. We currently have seven different varieties, surrounded by lilac, honeysuckle, lavender, and more

I have once again digressed from my story, something I'd like to say is an anomaly, but would better be described as defining personality trait. This is how a simple conversation over breakfast turned into hours of talking about our hopes and dreams for the future.

Earlier, I shared with you how camping each year at Mosey Wood was a big part of Andrea's youth. She also came back in her early teen years to work in the camp kitchen for an entire summer. Had her life not taken the unexpected twists and turns that it did, there's a strong likelihood she'd have returned for quite a few more summers. She might even have remained active with the camp into the present, like her friend, Thunder.

Thunder is a fantastic example of what I previously mentioned about God letting us know when we're on the right track, giving an indication that we're meant to be exactly where we are. She's not just Andrea's friend, she was also her counselor at Mosey Wood. Much of my wife's love for camping was fostered under the guidance of Thunder and her fellow counselors.

It was a formative time in her life and as the years passed, Andrea came to realize that like me, she felt closest to God in nature. Unfortunately, she found less time to enjoy nature as life got in the way. Prior to our meeting each other in that serendipitous moment at the call center, Andrea had fallen prey to the bane of adulthood.

She worked long hours to pay her bills, trading her free time for the challenges of single motherhood. Money was tight, so she did what she could to make ends meet, often going without so that her children, my future stepchildren, would always have what they needed. She rarely had time for a social life and lost contact with her friends from camp, a memory that seemed far too distant.

Meanwhile, about a year before I met Andrea, I went out on a date with a girl named Mary Jo. We had met in an online chat room and began talking about mutual interests, sharing our common frustrations with our lives. Eventually, we decided to go out to dinner and see if there was any kind of connection beyond a friendship.

Long story short, there was not. Mary Jo was a nice girl and a great conversationalist, but I realized almost immediately, that I was not in a place to date anybody. We did enjoy some good discussions and she told me all about her love of the outdoors. She shared memories of a Girl Scout camp she had attended and later returned to as a counselor.

By the end of the evening, it was clear that we were different people who wanted different things. I drove her back to her house and we shared an awkward goodbye, before I quickly sped away. It was an unpleasant drive home for me, because each one of my insecurities seemed to be dancing a jig in my brain. I decided I was done with dating and I never expected to see or talk to her again.

Clearly, I was wrong about being done with dating and as it turned out, I was also wrong about the rest. When I told Andrea the story of that date, I was greeted by a combination of raucous laughter and jokes about my age. She eventually tired herself out and stopped, telling me that the girl I knew as Mary Jo was also her childhood camp counselor, Thunder.

Andrea's delight over my awkwardness was only increased a few years later, when we took my oldest daughter, Elizabeth, for her first stay at Camp Mosey Wood. In the gift shop at the main lodge, we encountered Thunder, and I tried (unsuccessfully) to hide behind a postcard rack.

I desperately looked around for an escape and saw Andrea struggling to keep it together. I thought she was going to either pee herself or burst a blood vessel from trying so hard to contain her laughter at my predicament. The adult thing to do would have been to walk over and say hello, then apologize for not calling. Instead, I chose that postcard rack and Thunder eventually walked away.

The icing on the cake came a few years later, not long after we moved to Nazareth. Guess who moved into our neighborhood, less than a block away from our house? Yup. She had gotten married and was happy, something I probably would have learned that day at camp, if I hadn't been so embarrassed and actually talked to her.

God surely does have a sense of humor and one day as I was getting the mail, I turned around and came face to face with her. I looked in vain for a postcard rack, but we'd never installed one in the front yard, so I mustered up the courage to say hello. I wasn't sure if she was going to return the greeting or tell me to go stick my head in a beehive.

To my great relief, she couldn't have been friendlier and while it was obvious she recognized me from what was probably the worst date of her life, she was kind enough not to bring it up. We talked briefly, before she continued on her way. The next time I saw her walking, I said hello again and Andrea came out and greet her too.

Thunder and her family moving into our neighborhood turned out to be a great blessing for everyone. I believe we both found some closure, Andrea and Thunder reconnected over their many shared memories, and they became good friends. Prior to Andrea's teaching at our church's preschool, she helped with childcare for Thunder's young daughter.

Some might chalk that whole experience up to coincidence, but I disagree. I see it as God letting us know things were unfolding according to his exquisite plan. We all had free will to do whatever we pleased and could have made choices that would have changed everything. I know there have been many times in my life where I regretted making certain decisions, but had I never made those fumbles and endured the consequences, I wouldn't have ended up here.

When I consider the disparity between God's plan and free will, I don't see either as mutually exclusive. I believe God's plan for our life is conceived long before we are, created by a collaboration between our soul and our creator. He knows us better than we know ourselves and that diagram of our life includes the different choices he anticipated us making, both good and bad. As lost as I may feel at any given time, God knows where I am and more importantly, He knows where I'm going.

God's plan for me was in the forefront of my mind throughout our visit to the inn and that last breakfast we enjoyed on the veranda was a perfect example. The conversation that unfolded throughout the different courses was exactly what I needed.

Andrea and I shared a table with an amiable couple named Bonnie and Louis, who seemed about the same age as us. We had talked to them in passing the previous day, meeting on the landing between the first and second floor of the inn. They were heading to explore a local park and hiking trail, followed by a wine tasting tour.

One of our favorite aspects of a B&B stay is the interaction with other guests. We've met some tremendous people over the years and a few, well, memorable folks. One time over breakfast at a B&B in Cape May, a gentleman regaled everyone at the table with the most fanciful story of partying at his friend's apartment the night before Thanksgiving. There were windows looking out towards the Museum of Natural History and they could watch the enormous balloons being inflated for the Macy's Thanksgiving Day Parade.

He mentioned that his dentist friend throws a party each year and went into great detail. Apparently one year, there was some sort of commotion and a little statue had been knocked out of the window. It landed on one of the balloons and punctured it, causing the whole thing to deflate.

If that story sounds familiar, it's because he stole it from an episode of Seinfeld. He legitimately told the story to a table of strangers, under the assumption that we'd never seen the show. It was like a dinner theater monologue, performed by a lousy actor with odd mannerisms, while eating stuffed French toast.

Thankfully, Louis and Bonnie were nothing like that and the conversation flowed as if we'd known each other for years. Louis talked about his job as an engineer, driving trains for NJ Transit, which I thought sounded fascinating. Bonnie did some kind of market research, organizing focus groups from an office in their home.

I'm a little embarrassed to say it, but I didn't completely understand everything Bonnie mentioned doing, although I nodded my head and put on a good show. The part that did catch my attention was when she mentioned working from home. Louis had told me the day before, they live in a log cabin not too far from my hometown.

They found a company that specifically builds log cabins, customized the plans with everything they wanted, and it was built four years ago on a secluded, wooded property.

From his description, both the house and his property sounded gorgeous.

Andrea and Bonnie were talking when you brought over the coffee and Louis made a joke about finally being able to enjoy coffee without crayons melted in the pot. They had a little guy at home named John, who was the same age as our Angelica, and it seems he takes great pleasure in dunking his crayons in their coffee.

We don't have that problem, though the kids sure do love pushing our buttons. Just this afternoon, Joseph walked past me holding one of my hammers and when I asked him what he was doing, he replied, "Oh, you'll see…"

I immediately sent him back to the garage to put it away and he got all grumpy. As he was walking down the steps, I heard, "I guess you don't like when some people try to do nice things for other people in this house." That compelled me to step in again and address the smart mouth, which was the precise moment Angelica chose to creep up behind me like a ninja and shrieked that she had to go pee. I nearly fell down the stairs.

Those kids drive me absolutely crazy and I'm relatively sure they do it on purpose most of the time, but they and their mother are my entire world. It's like I told Louis, my two stepchildren have a father who loves them and will always be there for them. That doesn't affect my own love for Alex and Liz, or my desire to be there for them, but if something should happen to me, they'll still have their father and I know they will be ok.

For my three biological children, I'm the only dad they'll ever get. I cut each of their umbilical cords, held them when they were still fresh from the factory, and in that delivery room, I made them a promise. I pledged to dedicate my life to making theirs better, both in the present and long after I'm gone.

Bonnie and Louis nodded in agreement and Bonnie said they feel the same way about John. Originally, they had hoped for a large family, but as Bonnie explained while I was trying to enjoy my quiche, Louis has a very low sperm count and multiple doctors told them they were very lucky to have John.

Now, I have compassion for their situation, but the sperm count thing took me by surprise and she said it as casually as someone might talk about the weather. I had to fight back the laughter and when I saw the look of disdain on Louis's face, I nearly spit my quiche all over Andrea. In an attempt to recover, I put my hand over my mouth and pretended I was coughing.

I think they bought it, because Louis's face turned as red as the strawberries you served us and he stared off toward the fountain. Meanwhile, Bonnie continue to talk about their son, showing us pictures she kept on her phone. For what it's worth, Louis's solitary swimmer who defied the odds must have been a good one, because that John is one cute kid.

The rest of breakfast continued without any further talk of bodily fluids and I distracted Louis by pointing out the waterfall in the distance. We picked the same table as the day before and it's positioned perfectly to see the falls clearly through a gap in the trees. Andrea told Bonnie about her "Birthday Buddy" and how holding your grandson made her feel so much better about not being there to hold the baby in the hospital.

It was a great way to wind up our trip and just as we were all getting up to leave, Bonnie stopped, looked at me, and sat back down. I froze, sort of halfway up and halfway down, looking between her and then Andrea, trying to figure out what to do.

Bonnie continued to gaze at me as if she was mulling something over in her head, so I sat down and asked if she was ok. I didn't notice at the time, but Louis had distracted Andrea and gotten her away from the table.

She replied that she was fine, but she wondered how I was doing. Bonnie explained that she had seen me on the first evening of our stay, when I had come downstairs in the middle of the night. It seems she couldn't sleep either and didn't want to wake up Louis, so she had come down to the kitchen to read.

I never saw her that night; I thought I was alone. The problem with that, Billie, is that when I'm alone and there's something on my mind, I talk out loud to try and work my way through it. It's more of a whisper rather than a normal speaking voice, but it helps me to speak the thoughts aloud. What this all means is Bonnie had heard everything I said.

She heard me talking about my struggles with panic disorder, GAD, depression, and PTSD. I talked about what

I experienced, how it felt, and went into details I never shared with anyone outside of my doctor's office, plus a few things even he doesn't know. This whole trip had been one colossal, yet cathartic release of pain, so when I thought I was alone, I didn't hold anything back.

After she told me this, I felt inconceivably exposed, more so than if I were completely naked in the middle of a crowded city street. It didn't matter that just one person had heard me, because I didn't know this person. I knew nothing of any substance about who she was, yet she knew so much about me. My deepest secrets had been exposed and there was nothing I could do about that.

It felt like time had stopped. I saw nothing and nobody but Bonnie, as I stared at her face and tried to figure out how I was supposed to respond. This woman knew the intimate details of what happened on the night I put a loaded pistol in my mouth and planned to end my life. There was nothing I could say to her that would change anything or take it back.

Bonnie continued, noting she wanted to give me privacy, but the only way she could have gotten back to her room was through the parlor where I was sitting. She said she considered going outside, but it was very dark out and she figured I would hear the door anyway. I was still at a complete loss for words, mortified that this stranger knew my darkest secrets. All I could do was continue to stare in disbelief and horror.

She leaned in closer to me and I wondered what else I was about to hear. Had she seen me crying by the lake, too? As she opened her mouth to speak, I did my best to brace myself for what was coming next. She said,

"My father shot himself in our backyard when I was 10 years old."

Bonnie went on to tell me her father had struggled with alcohol and depression for most of his life. When he was in college, Bonnie's father was drunk and got in a car accident that stole the life of his best friend. She knew he took medicine and went to counseling, but it didn't help him.

Bonnie began to cry as she told me how mad she had been at her father since it happened, because she couldn't comprehend why he would do that to her mom, brothers, and her. Bonnie revealed that until she sat in that kitchen and listened to the things I was saying, she never understood how deeply her father had been suffering.

She explained how she heard the words I was speaking but imagined them coming from her father. It was so vivid that she felt like she could actually hear his voice coming through at times. She never realized how much he had been hurting, or that her father probably was thinking of her and her family when he took his life. He wasn't in his right mind and likely believed he was doing them all a favor, just as I did.

We were both crying by that point and I stood up to hug Bonnie, with every ounce of the shame and humiliation I had felt, suddenly gone. All I wanted was to comfort this woman who no longer felt like a stranger. When Bonnie hugged me back, she held on tight, put her chin on my shoulder, and whispered, "Thank you."

I looked over at Andrea and found her standing with Louis by the dining room window, tears running down both their faces. She later told me that Louis had initially gotten her away from the table by pretending to drop something and asking for her help to find it. Once they were far enough, he shared with Andrea what Bonnie was talking to me about.

I'm not sure if you happened to look out the window and see all the crying, Billie, but if you did, please know that those were not tears shed in sorrow. They were the result of God's grace washing away decades of pain from two strangers, each of whom were used as unwitting saviors, answering the other's prayers.

## Chapter 14

Following that surreal experience, Andrea and I went back up to the room to decompress; The whole thing was intensely emotional and powerful to the point that I was in a foggy daze. I don't remember much of what we talked about in the room, not because it wasn't important, but because I was still trying to process what had happened.

 I do remember her asking if I was ok and not knowing the answer at first. I felt exhausted and emotionally drained, but at the same time, there was a feeling that I can only equate with what someone must experience when they've been held captive for years and are finally released.

There was a sense of freedom, but also perplexity and apprehension. My initial response to her question was one of my own, "Did that really just happen?" She reassured me that it had, put her arms around me, and I began to weep. I had been so positive that if anyone ever knew my deepest and darkest secrets from some of the worst times in my life, they would judge me and hate me, just as I had judged and hated myself all these years.

Those tears were born of neither sadness, nor happiness. They were an embodiment of internal liberation and intense, purgative release. Not only did Bonnie not think that I was a terrible person, but hearing about my worst moments actually helped her. All that internal hatred and shame seemed to be gone and I didn't know how to feel.

I had known pain and psychological constraint for so long, I was entirely unaccustomed to living without it. "I'm ok,"

I finally responded, excusing myself and heading into the bathroom to straighten up. A quick glance in the mirror turned into a prolonged stare. I surveyed myself as if I was looking at a different person. Andrea talked through the bathroom door and told me to go relax, while she packed our bags and took them down to the car.

Normally, I'd protest and continue to help pack up the room, but still deep in thought, I blindly followed her direction. I walked down the stairs and into the parlor area next to the main foyer where everything was quiet.

Spotting that same high back leather chair where I sat and watched the storm on our first day, I walked over and took a seat, peering out the window. The sun was shining and the fountains in the pool were reflecting its light with a kaleidoscope effect, like streams of liquid prisms, sending tiny rainbows in all directions. Looking up, I saw a deep, cerulean sky with occasional puffs of white.

The storm had passed, I thought to myself, as a smile formed on my face. Those clouds in my brain were dissipating and I began to realize that after all these years, it was over. The anguish I had held inside for so long, the pain that had come to define me, and the shame which blocked any sense of joy from reaching beyond the surface of my being… it was finally gone. The storm had passed indeed!

A sparkle caught my eye from the adjoining ballroom and I decided to go take a look. I sauntered into that stately, commodious space, greeted by shimmers of light dancing on the oak floorboards, beneath the ornate cut-glass chandeliers. It was if they were putting on a show just for me, and my smile broadened.

As I stood in the middle of that room, I thought back to my prior conversation with Andrea about what it must have been like in there when the inn was a private residence. Then, I thought about all the weddings and other joyous events that had been held in that space over the years, following the conversion to a B&B. I sat on the bench seat by the window for a few minutes and closed my eyes, trying to intuit the energy of the room.

What I felt was a strong sense of peace and love, as if the room had absorbed all that joy over the years, like an ethereal sponge, holding on to all the good memories. I could also tell that while I may have been the only one breathing in that room, I was definitely not alone.

The presence was a calming and friendly one, though I had no indication of who might have been there with me. I considered the man who had built the house, maybe a member of one of the families who lived there, or even one of your guests who checked out, but chose not to leave. I didn't know, but I spoke out loud to whoever was with me, thanking them for the peace that I had come to find during our stay.

I expected no response and received none, yet I was deeply appreciative nonetheless. I felt the need to thank God for the extraordinary blessing he had granted me. It didn't feel right to pray while sitting on the window seat, so I looked around the room and my gaze stopped at the giant fireplace.

The open hearth seemed like as good a place as any, so I made my way over there, got down on my knees, and interlaced my fingers together. I meant to give a quick prayer of thanks but ended up talking for several minutes and I strongly felt like he was with me and heard every word.

I figured Andrea had decided to give me a little space, so I sort of wandered around and did my best to absorb it all while I still could. I passed through that parlor and into the brilliant dining room. What some might consider minutiae, I see as character and a precise attention to detail by the builder.

From the stained-glass transom panels and amber window shades to the giant stone fireplace and hand-carved wood trim that surrounded it, I could tell that great pains were taken in the design of this room. While I stood in there, my mind reached back to the pictures of the fire that had destroyed the original south wing, back in the 1920s.

In my head, I compared the pictures of the fire and the layout of the inn today, realizing the lost wing must have extended from that very room and the adjoining kitchen. I'm sure it was a grand addition to the house and fit in well with the rest of the building that was saved, but frankly, I felt that the room was perfect the way it was.

I saw a certain symmetry between that floor to ceiling stone fireplace on one wall and the three floor to ceiling windows on the other. Plus, the fireplace had that extraordinary feature of a window just above the mantle, which allowed me to stand in the middle of the room and see both the north and south grounds of the Trakehner Inn at the same time.

It's always fascinated me how masons can do that, curving the chimney vents around the window and then rejoining them above it. A straight path seems the only logical choice, but the smoke finds its way through those curves and the detour allows for the creation of something beautiful.

One particular feature in that room captured my interest the moment I saw it and throughout our stay, I went out of my way to keep coming back to it. I'm talking about the baroque metal baptismal font by the fireplace. You had mentioned your husband stumbled upon it and the font came from a church that was demolished.

Each time I looked at it and touched the dove, lamb, and the other symbols of Christ, I couldn't help but think of all the children who were brought into the faith from the blessed waters once contained within its basin. Touching the cross on top, I could feel the love emanating from that Holy relic.

There is no doubt that God is present in your home, of that I'm absolutely sure. I felt it when we arrived, I spoke to him throughout our visit, and experienced his profound grace, as he answered my deepest prayer and used me to fulfil the intensely personal prayer of another. What I couldn't understand is why He had done that for me?

I stood there in your dining room, staring at that baptismal font, wondering why God had chosen to give this staggering gift to me, when others deserved it so much more. The emotions from breakfast had begun to subside and my rational mind leapt into action. I tried asking him directly, but there was no response.

I never intended to come to Trakehner Inn and find God, and I surely didn't expect to find salvation in the Poconos. The trip was never supposed to be about me. I came there because I wanted to give my wife a birthday gift that would bring her serenity. I wanted to return Andrea to the same kind of lakefront wilderness environment that captured her heart when she was a young girl.

Yes, my life had been difficult and I'd faced obstacles, but so had Andrea. If you knew half of the pain and indignity she's had to endure over her life, you would agree that she deserved to be the one granted a reprieve. Beyond all of that, raising five children has not been easy and downright thankless at times, while her marriage to me brought a series of trials that neither one of us anticipated in the beginning.

Billie, I haven't lived the pious live of someone who deserves the blessings that have been given to me. I always assumed the challenges from my disabilities were God's way of balancing it all out. He led me to an amazing wife, gave me the greatest children any father could ever have the privilege to raise, and he made my dreams come true. At the same time, he worsened my disabilities so that I could never fully appreciate any of it, because I became wrapped up in my own pain and focused on struggling to keep my head afloat.

I believed I deserved that fate, because while I never intended to hurt anyone, it still happened when I spoke without thinking or acted impetuously, without considering the consequences. I never expected to be absolved from the hurt I had caused other people or the suffering they faced because of me.

So many thoughts flooded my mind as I stared at the cross atop the baptismal font and I turned away from it, walking into the kitchen. You were in one of the rooms of the north wing and I could hear you coming towards me, so I slipped out the back door to try and come to terms with the conflict in my head.

Right about that point is when Andrea found me and asked if I had checked out. I looked at her for a second, not grasping what she meant, before I caught myself and told her I hadn't, but you were right inside. Then I held the door open for Andrea, but she motioned for me to close it.

Andrea asked if I wanted to walk down to the lake one more time and I jumped at the opportunity. I thought maybe if I went to the place I felt God's presence the strongest, He would answer me, or at least lead me in the right direction to find some sort of understanding.

As we walked down the path to the lake, Andrea thanked me for the birthday trip. I asked if she had enjoyed it and tried to indiscreetly ascertain if she had found any kind of relief herself. She told me the trip had been exactly what she needed, a break from the real world.

That's great, I thought, but not God-answering-your-prayers great. I tried to pick her brain some more, but either my questions were all going right over her head, or she was purposely being evasive. That was a possibility, I considered, because Andrea is a private person about certain things.

Once we reached the fence near the lake, Andrea gestured to the falls and I told her to lead the way. We walked onto the pedestrian bridge next to the dam and took in the majesty of the water pouring over it, thundering to the bottom in rhythmic succession. At home, we use a white noise machine each night to sleep, but the digitally-recreated rushing water can't compare to the real thing.

Standing before those falls, holding Andrea's hand, I summoned up my courage to ask God the question that was eating me up inside. Before I could ask anything, I received an answer.

"Andrea" the voice responded in my brain, clear as the sky above us. That's all there was, just her name.

I told God I didn't understand. My question was about Andrea. Why God had chosen me instead of her… or virtually anyone else. Why weren't their prayers answered when mine were? I know Bonnie found her grace, but what about the billions of other people in the world? Why did He choose me?

"Andrea" the voice repeated.

Still confused, I looked over at Andrea. She was quietly watching the water rush under the bridge below us, holding onto my hand, blissfully unaware of my perplexing internal conflict with the almighty. She caught my glance and smiled, saying the water looked pretty.

I stared at her for a second, trying to figure out if there was something different that I hadn't noticed. She scrunched her eyes the way she used to when she was being playful, then she laughed and looked back at the water.

It took a few seconds to sink in, but then it hit me. I hadn't seen Andrea that happy in years. Granted, there were no kids asking her a million questions or St. Bernards whining to go out, but that wasn't it. I began to think of all the things we had done in the last few days, walking hand in hand around the property, having lunch at a local café, walking together to the lake, playing games in the parlor, joking around by the pool, going out to dinner, and sitting together to watch the sunset.

I asked Andrea if she had prayed for anything while we were there and she smiled coyly at me, before telling me that was between her and God. I tried to pressure her into answering and she mockingly asked if I was writing a book. I told her that as a matter of fact I was. It was titled, "Prayers that Andrea made to God" and I was stuck on chapter six.

"Good luck with that" she said and laughed, as she dropped my hand and strode away from the bridge, heading over to the stone fence at the edge of the inn property. Andrea sat down on the flat stone and I followed, sitting next to her.

I decided to just lay it all out for my wife and told her basically everything I wrote to you above. I watched the smile on her face change to more of a pensive look, as she sat there and patiently listened to everything I had to say. When I was done, Andrea said she had two questions for me.

"First, what makes you think God didn't answer one of my prayers?" she asked. I screamed in my head, since she had refused to answer that very question just seconds earlier, but kept it cool and calm on the exterior. I nicely asked her again if she had any answered prayers. She sarcastically made me promise not to put it in my book, before getting serious and leaning in close to me. Then she whispered in my ear, "It's none of your business."

"Really?" I uttered, as she broke out in laughter. Andrea told me she prayed for me to pee my pants and I said the joke was on her, because that didn't happen. "Yet..." she replied.

Then she got serious and asked if I really believed God took it all away, the panic, depression, PTSD and everything else. I told her I didn't know and talked about how relaxed I had felt throughout this entire trip. I said maybe he did take it all away and she interrupted me saying, "I hope not."

I was a little shocked by her response and she saw it in my face, so Andrea quickly followed up by saying that without those struggles, I wouldn't be me. She wanted me to feel better and be able to enjoy more of life, but those challenges and the pain are a part of me. She said they made me the person that she fell in love with, married, and chose to be the father of her children.

Andrea continued, clarifying that she would love it if I never had another panic attack and found a way to suffer less from my other conditions, but she'd never want them to be completely gone. "You struggle every day, but you never give up and you never lose faith. That's one of the things I love about you."

I thanked her and before I got all the words out, she interrupted me again. "You need to stop that, too. Stop thanking me for telling you how I feel. I wouldn't say it if it weren't true. You have a gift for looking at the world and seeing things other people don't, but when you look in the mirror, you can't see all the good things the rest of us do."

She was on a roll, "You are an excellent husband and father, and you come up with these elaborate dreams that seem impossible to everyone else, then you make them happen. Think about everyone you helped with Donate My Weight, all those fundraisers you started to help other families, the books you've written, the museum exhibits you've created... Your college invited you back to be the keynote speaker. You are a force to be reckoned with and everyone sees that but you."

I started to respond, but Andrea stopped me and asked, "Have you done it yet?"

"Have I done what?" I countered.

She asked, "Have you done what God brought you here to do?"

The question stumped me, and I had no idea what she meant. Throughout this entire weekend, I'd revisited memories that I hoped to never think about again. I rediscovered parts of my soul I thought were long gone, I'd grown closer to God than I had ever been, and I even served as a conduit for His divine grace, helping to answer the decades-old prayer of a little girl who grew up without her dad. Which one did Andrea mean?

I must have been staring at her for an inordinate amount of time as I tried to work it all out in my head, because she waved her hands in front of my eyes and said, "Hello?"

"Oh, sorry…" I said, trailing off, "I just don't know what you mean."

"You still don't get it? Why do you think God brought you here?" she asked, with frustration creeping into her voice.

"I don't know what you want me to say," I answered, beginning to get annoyed myself.

"Ben! Think about everything that's happened this weekend. Can't you see that God is trying to help you? He brought you here, he spoke to you, he showed you your purpose in life. Do you realize how rare that is? Do you understand how many people would give anything to know why they're here? God's doing everything he can to bring you peace, but he can't give you forgiveness!" she yelled.

"What?!?!" I shouted back. "I thought God DID forgive me! Wasn't that what this morning was all about?!?!"

"YOU NEED TO FORGIVE YOURSELF!" Andrea screamed at me, before lowering her voice and finishing. "God has forgiven you, but you need to find a way to forgive yourself."

In that moment, I felt like I did the day I met her. Andrea had stunned me again and I didn't know what to say. I just stared out over the lake, until I felt her take my hand in hers, leading me towards the inn. Once we reached the veranda, she turned and kissed me. Then, without a word, she went inside to give you our key and check out of Trakehner Inn.

I walked over to the pool, looked down at my reflection, and thought about what Andrea said.

# Chapter 15

Andrea and I have been together for nearly 13 years and in all that time, we've never travelled anywhere without some sort of issue related to my disabilities or one of my conditions getting in the way. Panic attacks can happen any time and any place, and like I mentioned before, they've caused us to abandon long-awaited trips and come home. Agoraphobia has turned me into a prisoner in my own home, rarely going out or doing anything beyond a small circle around our house. When I do leave, it's with persistent and severe anxiety, along with the strong sensation that the world is closing in around me.

The PTSD brings a constant need be alone and I get startled or upset easily, which inevitably turns into a series of irrational arguments. A person in that state says things that hurts others, things they can never take back. GAD makes traveling a nightmare, because there are dangers and concerns everywhere, and I am always worrying about the money we spend, along with the welfare of any loved ones who aren't with us.

Depression feels like a heavy blanket of morose woe, smothering me and sapping my energy. Have you ever tried to walk in thick mud that creates a suction to your shoes and seems to grab your feet with every step? Picture that sensation on a sweltering hot day with oppressive humidity. Every step brings fatigue and frustration, and a strong compulsion to give up. That is what it feels like to live with depression.

As you can imagine, I'm not the ideal travelling companion and even when we go to places like Cape May, where I've vacationed since I was a baby and have travelled hundreds of times throughout my life, it never goes away or gets any easier. I love Cape May like I do my own hometown, but I struggle there, just as much as I do in my local community. The one exception to that miserable rule has been our stay at Trakehner Inn.

Your home evoked a tranquility I'd not felt since I was a boy. Despite this being my first visit to Trakehner Inn, there was a strong sense of familiarity that's difficult to explain and I've never felt as close to God as I did when I was there. I was glad to hear Andrea checked us out, because I wasn't looking forward to turning over that room key.

I'd walked up from the pool and met her in the dining room, just in time to say goodbye to you, before you headed out to take care of some errands. Andrea suggested we take one last walk through of the inn before we went home. We headed over to the kitchen, admiring that beautiful stone floor on the south side of the room. I noticed it was the same stone that's around the giant fireplace in the front parlor and figured it was original to the house.

Walking on the stones, I could tell they were textured and bumpy in areas, not perfectly flat like the engineered stone products of today. That's the kind of old-school character you can't find in a modern home and it evoked memories of the walls at Nana and Grandpa's house.

Andrea really liked the look of the kitchen, with all the wood paneling that matched the cabinets and the hardwood floors in the main area. The red-tiled backsplash and counters offset it well, especially with that giant square island in the center.

When I looked at your island, my imagination ran wild. I envisioned it being used to prepare hundreds of hors d'oeuvres for a big party, covered with all different varieties of freshly baked Christmas cookies, or maybe a buffet of dinner items for a big family gathering.

Another favorite of ours was the antique wood burning stove in your kitchen's red brick alcove. I love that it was installed where the original cooking stove would have been, blending the past with the present. I could picture the flames emanating from red embers inside it, throwing off heat on a cold winter's day.

We walked around the downstairs of the north wing and passed through one door leading to an area that seemed as if it would have made an ideal family room. There was a nice stone fireplace, built-in bookshelves on the wall, and a gorgeous view out a huge leaded-glass window that faces the Tudor style exterior around the front door area. Andrea and I both agreed, the more we saw of this house, the more it felt like we were wandering through a fairy tale.

While we were in there, I noticed some personal things on the table and Andrea saw a baby swing for your grandson, which made us think we'd encroached upon your personal space. Sorry about that, Billie, we never would have done it on purpose. Still, though, it was a pretty great room.

Heading upstairs to look around, we saw the three beautiful bedrooms and imagined owning the house ourselves. Andrea thought they would be perfect for family and friends to come visit us and we could even transform the common area into a fourth bedroom, to have more room for our loved ones to stay.

I joined in the fun, saying we should use the Presidential Suite in the south wing as our master bedroom, and the other four bedrooms over there would be perfect for our children. The room we'd wandered into that seemed to be your private area, with the bookshelves and fireplace, would make the quintessential family room. The adjoining spaces could be a tremendous office for me and sewing room for Andrea, who currently completes her sewing projects in a little corner of our basement.

We headed back downstairs and as we walked through the kitchen, everything seemed to take on a different feeling. I looked at it through my mind's eye and started blending what was in front of me with our own kitchen at home. Andrea wondered aloud whether we needed the three ovens and multiple dishwashers you used to cater to your guests. Probably not, we figured

She also noticed the old walk-in cooler was still there, though it was now used for storage. Looking at the vintage handle made me think back to the early days, when this house was a retreat for the original owner's family and friends. I couldn't help but wonder how many fish and wild game were stored in there after those early 1900s hunting sessions.

Teddy Roosevelt was an avid hunter and frequent visitor here, so it was likely this cooler once held Presidential conquests. As I was going on about the history to my wife, she interjected that it would make a great laundry room. Yes, we could absolutely wash our underwear in the same space where President Roosevelt once stored the fruits of his hunting prowess.

On our way back to the parlor, Andrea stopped in the dining room and said she would want to buy all the furnishings and keep everything the way it was. "Yes, Mrs. Rockefeller," I thought to myself, putting numbers together in my head, as if we had even the remotest possibility of actually being able to do this.

I was about to share the total I approximated when she interjected that there were two things from our current home that she couldn't do without. I was intrigued and assumed she didn't mean the dogs.

"I could never leave those tables behind," Andrea said, referring to our kitchen and dining room tables, which were both handmade by a carpenter in our area. I bought them for her on our anniversary last year and the kitchen table was built specifically for our family, following a brainstorming session between Andrea and the carpenter.

She had always longed for a true family dinner table that was our own and not some hand-me-down or yard sale purchase like the previous ones. Andrea wanted a place where we could eat our meals together and make all kinds of special memories as the years went by, then pass it down to our children.

When we first visited the carpenter at his home, he went over different options for Andrea to consider, showing us samples of his work, which included a 10-foot-long dark walnut table he had made for his own family. It was their first Thanksgiving and all the relatives were coming to celebrate. He and his wife had no place to seat everyone, so he built that table specifically for the occasion.

Afterwards, they continued to use one small part of it for family meals, but it took up almost the entire room and they were looking to downsize. I talked to him discreetly when Andrea wasn't around and bought that one too. I knew it would make the perfect dining room table for our own family and would be big enough to one day seat our children's spouses and our grandchildren.

I told Andrea that I agreed with bringing the tables and then we made our way back to the parlor, admiring that giant fireplace that flanked the dual staircase. It was Andrea's turn to be sentimental as she envisioned a scene with our children's wet coats, gloves, and hats drying by the crackling logs, while we all played a board game together in the parlor. That did sound pretty great.

We headed into the grand ballroom and I swear, I could actually see the couches on either side of the lit fireplace, the leather wingback chairs in the corner, and our daughter Kateri, playing "Silent Night" on that elegant baby grand piano. Andrea said she could envision Joseph barreling down the stairs, with our saints closely behind him, all eager to run outside and play in the snow.

Andrea and I are both huge fans of the Christmas season, along with the sense of joy and goodwill that pervades the air during the month of December. One of my favorite parts of the final walk-through was the discussion we had about bringing our extended families together, to come celebrate Christmas in this magical home. That's a personal dream I've had for a long time.

Every part of the house would be adorned with fresh pine garland, hundreds of family decorations, and several trees set up throughout. Andrea joked that the place would look like the North Pole each year and I told her it absolutely would. I spoke of Christmas songs perpetually playing at low volume throughout the downstairs and the air, thick with classic holiday scents like balsam, bayberry, apple cinnamon, or peppermint.

We agreed that outside, the stables would be full again. We'd board the horses Andrea had longed for since her childhood and those from neighbors, who needed a place to stable their steeds. The garage would be a mixture of storage, a workshop for me to tinker in peace, and space for the van.

That guest cabin on the property would make an excellent caretaker's house, so we could always ensure the building and grounds were kept in pristine condition. Andrea imagined welcoming the neighbors over at different points of the year and I thought a giant block party would be wonderful on the south lawn.

The inn and surrounding property managed to encompass every single detail we had each dreamt about since we were children. From Andrea's fascination with hidden rooms and horse stables, to my affinity for stained glass and fireplaces in virtually every room, Trakehner Inn met the mark. This magnificent home achieved the seemingly impossible, combining my preferred look of stone and exposed wood with Andrea's predilection for a more contemporary style. It was uncanny.

The more we walked the halls and shared our visions for different spaces, the more I wanted every single bit of it. I wanted to raise my children in that house, to see my children raise their own children in that house, and to know that it would be passed through the generations long after Andrea and I were gone.

I knew how unrealistic it was to even consider this fairy tale home could be ours one day, but I still found myself thinking about it. I stood in the dining room and admired the baptismal font one last time, then smiled and turned towards the window. I looked down at the lake and imagined seeing it every morning when I woke up.

As I was pondering that wonderful prospect, I experienced a rapid flurry of short movies surging through my mind, one after the other. I barely had the chance to process each vignette, before it was replaced by the next. I was reliving different moments from the weekend, but through someone else's eyes, watching myself and feeling the emotions of the moment.

Suddenly, I saw hands reach out from the sides of my viewing frame, with arms enrobed in white cloth. The hands rested on my shoulders, though I didn't remember feeling any such sensation at the time. There was no chance to think it through, because I swiftly found myself watching a scene on the pedestrian bridge next to the dam. I observed myself standing on that bridge next to Andrea and I seemed to be looking around for something. Then, I heard a deep, soothing voice declare, "I am here."

"Wait!" I thought, as things started to click into place, but the video montage continued. I saw myself with Andrea on the veranda at sunset and the deer were there, playing in the yard. Next, we were lying in bed and talking the following morning, then sitting on the veranda at breakfast. I was shown my intense interaction with Bonnie and felt the raw power in that moment. When Bonnie and I hugged, I watched those arms come out from the sides again, this time reaching around the two of us in a big hug.

Through who's eyes am I seeing all of this? Surely it can't be... Before I could finish my thought, I saw Andrea and me, back on that bridge again. We were holding hands and she was looking down at the water below us, while I spoke to God in my mind, except I could hear the words as if I were saying them aloud.

Then, I heard the response in that same heartening voice, seeming to come from my own vantage point. It said, "Andrea." Next, I watched her yelling at me about forgiving myself, before being whisked to the side of the Trakehner Inn pool, where the final scene took place. I saw myself looking deep into my shimmering reflection in the pool water, then heard the words I expressed in my mind, "I forgive you."

Just as quickly as this weekend flashed before my eyes, the encounter ended, and I was back in the dining room. Everything became clear to me at that point. I had been correct when I believed I wasn't alone on the window seat earlier that morning. Jesus had been by my side the entire trip, holding me steady as I faced my demons, comforting me while I wept, and sharing my joy, as I experienced each of the revelations God had fashioned. It was His voice that I heard.

I knew that forgiving myself was the final step I had to take before I could fully experience the blessing of peace this trip had been about. My big mistake, however, was thinking it was all for me. Our trip had been meant to bring peace to several people and answer each of their prayers, including yours, Billie.

Your prayers are between you and God, though I strongly believe this whole experience was meant to address them. Knowing some of the loss you've endured and how, in even the most difficult of times, you've been a rock to those around you, it only makes sense. You never lost faith in God and I know in my heart, he's never lost faith in you, either.

While I walked out of that dining room and headed towards the front door, Jesus spoke to me one final time. He said, "Benjamin, I love you and believe in you. Now you must believe in yourself!"

Billie, as I write to you today, I am surer than ever that the Lord is not finished with me yet. The challenges from my disabilities returned almost immediately after we left Trakehner Inn and as powerful as I felt up there, the suffering continues to overwhelm me at times. What changed was my perspective.

I recognize that my marriage, the births of my children, and all the good I had been able to do for others was largely because of the way those disabilities had affected my life. I have also come to realize that I've never been closer to God than I was at the inn. What began as a little wind of faith has grown into a full-blown gale, and I now know where I belong.

Mark my words, Billie, the day will come when we turn that heavenly fairy tale into reality and take the keys to Trakehner Inn off your hands. Your peace is coming and just as your parents did fifty years ago, we'll write our own chapter in the history of this blessed building, making it our Miller family home.

Sincerely,

*Ben Miller*

9 780578 401430